FREEDOM BY THE CREEK

SUZANNE MARTIN

ACKNOWLEDGEMENTS

I want to thank my niece, Jessica Ly, for her help with the cover and for her inspiration and cheerleading in helping me to finish this long-awaited project.

DEDICATION

To my family and all those who read this book, thank you for supporting my dream of putting my imagination on paper.

PROLOGUE

"The cat is dead," he simply stated.

The words thundered through Kelly's ears like violent waves as her eyes widened in horror. She looked pleadingly to her mother for some sort of denial. Her mother, holding an infant in one arm, quickly wrapped her other arm around Kelly to pull her closer.

"You're sure?" she asked in desperation. "She's not just sick?"

He pursed his lips and sighed. "I'm sure." He looked at the little girl who had silent tears streaming down her tiny, pink cheeks. Her tangled, blonde waves jolted up and down upon her quivering shoulders. Pity fell over him and he looked back at the mother and softened his voice. "She's not sick. Her neck is broken." He waited a few moments.

"Any idea what might have happened?"

She adjusted the infant more comfortably in her arms and looked down with embarrassment. "No," she said and then paused as if to choose her words carefully. "She's a stray. My little girl's been caring for her. She has been hanging around the house for a while now and she's been feeding her. They have become inseparable. We found her in the driveway this morning like this. I didn't know what else to do."

By this time Kelly was crying audibly. Between choppy sobs, she managed to mutter, "You… can't… kick… cats."

He looked at her, puzzled, and just as he was about to question the remark, her mother quickly cut in.

"Well, we've wasted enough of your time. Just give me the bill and we'll be on our way."

Ignoring her, he took the cat and gently wrapped it in a large towel and carried it into an adjoining room. When he returned, he once again looked at the mother. She would not make eye contact with him. Instead, she kept her eyes focused on the floor and gently nestled her cheek upon the infant's head. Her long blonde strands draped the baby's head making it appear as if this tiny human had an oversized wig on that reached her dainty, bare feet. The sight was rather amusing to him, and he couldn't help but smile. She glanced up quickly to notice this and immediately gave him a frown before returning her gaze to the floor.

He looked at his watch and ran his fingers through his thick, chestnut hair. He should have been out the door half an hour ago. Rusty was home and probably had a path worn in the carpet by now. Never had he owned a dog that he was convinced could tell time. He assumed Rusty's history of abuse before he had taken over his care had caused this extreme OCD. But he loved the old Bloodhound, so he dealt with it.

"There is no charge," he finally stated.

She looked up at him abruptly. "No sir. I am not a charity case. I will take a bill," she demanded, but this time looked stubbornly into his eyes.

And it was at that moment that he noticed her eyes. Her beautiful, warm, blue eyes. Eyes so mesmerizing that he found it difficult to avert his stare. But there was also something alarming in those eyes. *Perhaps fear?*

When he finally found his voice again, he replied softly, "This is not charity, ma'am. I did nothing to help you."

She looked down at her daughter, who was finally calming down and then at the clock on the wall. She had less than half an hour to catch the last bus back home so there was no time to argue. She turned to him. "And will you take care of Dalila?"

He paused and then looked at her, confused, and asked, "You want me to take care of your *daughter*?"

"What?" she asked and looked to find a look of horror on Kelly's face. "My goodness, of course not!"

Realizing his mistake, he proclaimed with embarrassment, "Oh, of course! The cat! The cat's name is Dalila. Sorry, it's been a long day."

Her eyes softened and he could see a glimpse of a smile as she tried to suppress a chuckle.

"I will take very good care of Dalila," he stated and smiled as he looked at Kelly. Her small body had finally relaxed. She seemed like a sweet little girl. Even in the tattered clothes she wore, he could tell she was well cared for by this woman.

"You're new in town, I'm guessing?" he asked, returning his gaze to the mother.

"We are," she replied shyly.

"Well, just know that there are a lot of resources here in our town if you need *anything*." He glanced at the little girl and continued in a sweet, gentle voice, "And there's a really nice park just down the street from here. You can't miss it. In the summer, a field of daisies grows behind it that stretches for miles. So, of course, they named it Daisy Park."

Kelly's eyes finally lit up. "Do they have swings?"

"They have swings and slides and all kinds of fun things," he replied, happy to distract her from her sorrow.

Her mother glanced at the clock again, and then nervously said, "Well, thank you Dr…"

"Chris," he interrupted. "Please call me Chris." He held out his hand. "Miss…?"

She smiled shyly, took his hand, and softly answered. "Camille."

CHAPTER 1

It was the middle of August and the sun's brutal rays showed no mercy to the Owens family as they drove for what seemed like their thousandth mile down the endless road to their new life. The radio announced a scorching ninety-six degrees, which they considered an understatement, as they passed the *Welcome to New York* sign on the interstate.

The tan station wagon they traveled in had a broken air conditioner and only two of the four windows rolled all the way down. It was packed solid with the "necessities" that couldn't be jammed into the rental truck that was well on its way to greet them at their new home in Upstate New York.

Tommy Owens sat crunched in the back seat listening to his mother's soft chatter as she sat in the front seat, attempting to pile her sandy brown hair into a clasp. His father occasionally nodded in agreement with her as he tried to fuse the road signs with the map setting by his side.

Tommy shifted his knees for the hundredth time, silently cursing his inherited height. He took after his dad; he'd been told time and time again. All the way from his jet-black hair and brown eyes to his size twelve feet. He had his stubborn, or persistent, as he preferred to call it, personality as well. It showed in his school grades, the sports he played, and especially in his heart.

His mother Nancy, on the other hand, was lovingly passive in most cases. She was a kind and quiet woman, barely reaching five feet in height. Why, Tommy silently mused, couldn't his height have been more of a cross between the two? At least for the remainder of the drive.

"How much longer?" he asked, with a hint of annoyance.

"Not much," his father replied.

"Right," he mumbled and stared back out the window. He resented this whole idea of moving. He was perfectly happy back in Chicago with his friends, his school, and his girlfriend Tanya. He sighed and swallowed hard. Tanya was one of the prettiest girls he knew. He had spent his entire junior year trying to ask her out when finally on the last day of school before summer break, she finally said yes. And that was the beginning of a wonderful summer together filled with a mixture of both fun and discovery. She was his first girlfriend, and he was convinced, his last.

As he remembered their kiss good-bye, he looked hard at his parents. They were excited about the move. Pete had a "terrific" job waiting for him and Nancy was finally getting her home in the country. Oh, how he'd argued his point. He didn't think it was fair that he should spend his final year of high school with a bunch of strangers that were probably nothing like the kids he'd grown up with most of his life. But this was a once in a lifetime opportunity for Pete as the lead engineer in a new plant, and their minds were set. So, loving and respecting the both of them as he did, he reluctantly packed his bags. He would appease them for the time being, he thought, but come February he will be eighteen and an adult. And if things go as he hoped, he will head back to Chicago to finish out his senior year with Tanya and all his friends.

After a few more miles of driving, Pete announced that it was time for a restroom break and veered off the interstate and slowly rolled the car into a travel plaza.

Tommy sat upright. He didn't really feel the urge to go but was happy to have the chance to stretch his legs. After strolling around the parking lot for a few minutes, he went into the store and headed straight to the snack aisle. He grabbed a bag of chips, three candy bars, and a can of soda and quickly strode up to the register and placed them on the counter. The cashier, a lanky, red haired, young man with a smug expression, asked, "That it?"

Tommy nodded his head yes and just as the cashier was about to tally up his items, a slender hand reached around him and pushed the items aside. He turned to see Nancy juggling an apple, a container of yogurt, and a bottle of juice in her free arm. He rolled his eyes and sighed. She ignored him and pushed past him to put her items on the counter.

"We don't need these," she said to the cashier and pointed to the stuff that she had shoved to the side.

The cashier slowly rang up her items, placed them in a bag and deliberately handed them to Tommy with a smirk on his face. Tommy scowled at him, snatched the bag from his hand, and headed out of the store.

As he climbed back into the car, he thought about the patience it sometimes took concerning his mother. He was an only child, so she constantly fussed over his health and safety. He knew she had her reasons. After he was born, she had had numerous miscarriages until one year she was finally able to carry a baby to full term. It was ten years ago, but he remembered the day like it was yesterday. His grandparents had come to the house to care for him while his parents had gone to the hospital. After a long delivery, baby Bella was born. But Bella never came home. She had only lived for three days, and he was told that the angels had taken her to live with them. He remembered being incredibly angry and confused at the time and was left to wonder why his father didn't just take Bella back from the angels with his big, strong arms.

Bella had had a bedroom waiting for her at home. A room full of pinks and yellows that remained that way for all these years with the door closed. No one was allowed to enter that room and no one dared to speak her name again. As he got older, he understood more, and the sadness eventually ebbed. But not for Nancy. Still blaming herself, they would often catch her quietly sitting alone, consumed with sadness. A sadness that would sometimes last for days.

Nancy got back in the car and began to leaf through a travel brochure that she had grabbed while they waited for Pete. After a few more minutes, Pete finally made his way to the car, but instead of getting in the driver's seat, he opened Tommy's door and discreetly tossed a bag into him. When Tommy opened the bag, he was pleased to find the bag of chips and the three candy bars that Nancy had pushed aside. Pete got in the driver's seat, looked in the rearview mirror, and gave him a wink as he started the engine. Tommy smiled back and they were on the road again.

***

"You're going to love this place," Pete rambled on as Tommy stared out the window, watching the mile markers flash by. "It's perfect. There aren't any neighbors for at least two miles and there's a

3

big red barn sitting back behind the house. We could get a couple of horses to ride, too, Tom. Wouldn't that be great?"

"Sure," he answered, flatly, and reached for a candy bar. As he popped a piece of chocolate in his mouth, he closed his eyes and tried to imagine what was in store for him. The vision of a rooster sitting outside his window and waking him up with an annoying screech crossed his mind. He sighed deeply. *Yep, not going to be a taxi horn.*

After a few more hours of driving, Nancy spotted the sign and read out loud with excitement, "Welcome to Oxville!"

They turned off the interstate and onto a single laned road. Tommy quickly sat upright and looked around. The scenery exploded with endless trees and green, rolling hills scattered with pastures full of grazing cows and fields bursting with rows of corn. He looked around in awe and immediately felt humbled. *It really was beautiful.*

As they neared closer to town, he was mildly surprised to spot a bank and a post office right away. With a name like "Oxville", he had had his doubts.

"Well, at least it looks civilized," he muttered humorously and his parents both chuckled.

They proceeded to drive through town making sure to leave nothing unnoticed. It had almost a colonial look to it. Everything was kept and clean. The buildings had a look of fresh paint as if it had been done just for them. They eventually drove past the school and Tommy could not believe it was capable of holding an entire grade, let alone the whole high school.

They continued to absorb as much as they could until they reached the center of town when, just as they went through a traffic light, a sudden jolt and the sound of crunching metal caused Pete to slam on the brakes and squeal to an abrupt halt. A blue pickup truck had come out of nowhere and was now part of the wagon's hood ornament.

CHAPTER 2

Kelly Johnson was startled awake by the sensation of tiny claws scurrying across her chest. She quickly glanced downward in time to spot a little gray and white mouse burrow beneath her blanket and disappear. She sat up, pulled the musty blanket from her body and stretched off another bad night's sleep.

Although a tiny stream of light peered in through the back window, the basement was still very dark. She rolled off the sheetless mattress that laid upon the cold, cement floor and fumbled for a book of matches and a candle from an old crate that she used as her nightstand. Feeling like an old woman instead of the sixteen years that she was, she achingly lit the candle. A sinister glow spread across the basement and shadows immediately formed behind the wet clothes that hung on a clothesline stretching across the far side of the basement wall. The bouncing shadows created an eerie illusion of ghosts mocking her in dance. Off to the right, a beastly shadow from the towering furnace flickered about angrily, as if threatening to devour anything, *or anyone*, within its reach. And whatever might be lurking behind that furnace this morning was another frightening concern. *A monster? A ghost?* She shook her head and forced her gaze away to erase the unrealistic fears from her mind.

The surrounding walls were not much better. They were a hideous gray color that trickled with water in spots and patches of black clusters covered others. And then there was the odor. The faint scent of backed up septic hung in the air like a cloud that never seemed to melt away. It was all certainly a sore sight to wake up to, she thought and winced. One that she, no matter how much time had passed, could just not get used to.

With bare feet, she walked across the cold floor to the back window and reached up to push the curtains fully aside. A sigh of relief escaped her lips when the sun reached in to touch her face. *Good morning God.* She said the words in her head, as she did every morning. The heat spread across her face and warmed her inside. She closed her eyes and the memory that seemed to seep into her thoughts almost every morning filled her head.

"Higher!" she squealed, as Mother pushed her again. The swing went up even higher and she could feel the wind blowing through her

hair and her dress flapping up and over her thighs. As the swing reached its height, she stretched her toes out to desperately touch the cloud that was shaped like a bear. And as she swung back down, she could see Beth in her stroller, kicking her tiny feet and shrieking with delight. So many happy children playing and smiling. And Mother was there too, with the biggest smile of all. The excitement would continue until eventually she would feel her mother grasp at the chains slowly bringing her to a halt. And then the fun would end.

She thought of that park every morning and she knew she would never tire of it. And she remembered the field of daisies. So vivid in her mind that she could smell them. It was this, and the children, that gave her hope.

A stir from behind her snapped her from her thoughts and she looked back at the mattress that lay next to hers. She saw the two children, not awake yet, and pushed the curtains back together before walking over to check on them. They looked like angels, and she wished she could always see them like this. Billy and Beth were her life. They were about eight and ten years old, with Billy being the younger of the two. But anyone who might chance to see them would not have believed it. They were so small and thin. She bent down to brush a blond curl from Beth's face and gently put her hand on her forehead. It was warm again, as it had been for the past few days. Beth stirred and coughed hoarsely before turning her head away from Kelly to continue with her slumber.

They were both blond with big blue eyes, just like hers, and she knew she could easily pass as their mother. And of course that made sense. She *was* their mother for now. Until their real Mother returned to them for good.

Her mother had the same hair as well. She could remember that much. She closed her eyes again. This time to pray once again for the mother she missed so much and for her to return soon.

Billy woke up and looked at her.

"Is he gone yet?" he asked, eagerly.

"Shh...no, not yet," she whispered, and went over to sit on the mattress beside him.

"*Chaz!*" he exclaimed and then giggled as he reached his hand under his blanket to pull the squeaking mouse out.

Kelly put her finger to her lips to quiet him and then smiled. She didn't know where the name 'Chaz' came from, but she knew that he loved that mouse, and she figured the mouse was just as fond of him since he seemed to show up fearlessly every morning. Chaz would wait around patiently for any morsel of food and although Billy's own portions were usually limited, he would always manage to save him a crumb or two.

Beth woke and rubbed her eyes. "Is it raining, Kelly?" she asked groggily and coughed again.

"No, Honey, it's a nice day."

Both their faces lit up and they smiled. Their lives revolved around the sun and the rain. It defined their very existence.

Just then they heard the sound of heavy footsteps descending the basement stairs. The children stiffened and moved closer to Kelly.

"You better not burn the damn place down!" a big man bellowed when he reached the bottom of the stairs and tossed a large, green garbage bag on the floor.

Kelly guessed immediately that the bag was full of clothing. He would bring them down once in a great while and they would spend the morning sorting through them, picking out the things that were close to their sizes. They usually smelled of odd odors and carried stains, but they were happy to get the new clothes to keep up with their growing bodies.

He walked over slowly and deliberately and bent down to blow the candle out.

"You don't need this damn thing anyway," he grumbled and looked around before heading over to the back window. He stood for a moment and inspected the curtain. Kelly held her breath. As the silence lingered, she feared he might hear her heartbeat exploding in her chest since she could feel it pounding in her ears.

"Something interesting outside this morning?" he finally asked and glared at Billy.

Billy's eyes widened in fear.

"I did it," Kelly cut in, nervously. "They just woke up. I…"

"I didn't ask for lies," he interrupted, still looking at Billy. "Lies are for sinners and you know I don't tolerate sinners in my house."

As he moved closer to them, Chaz came out of nowhere and quickly scurried across his boot. He turned quickly and as he unsuccessfully tried to stomp on him, lost his footing and stumbled. The mouse ran off into the opposite side of the basement and disappeared. Kelly could tell that Billy wanted to laugh but knew better. They *all* knew better.

He huffed and with an angry glare in his eyes, bent down to stare into Billy's eyes. The closeness caused Kelly to wince. The scent that always seemed to follow him made her nauseous. It was a mixture of both heavy sweat and a strong, putrid, vinegar-like odor that poured from his skin, especially when he was at his angriest. His thick, dark hair was slicked back in obvious need of a wash and his blue work pants and white, stained t-shirt smelled of grease.

The intimidating stare continued until Billy dropped his gaze downward and fearfully whispered, "I'm sorry, Father."

He rarely looked at Kelly. Or Beth for that matter. She figured it was because although he hated them, he hated Billy the most. He always referred to him as the *Bastard Boy*. And perhaps he was hated more because of that. He was a boy. She did not know why. Or why he took the brunt of most of the beatings. Beatings that were so severe at times, that she would find herself jumping in the middle to protect his little body against this big mass of a man. But in the end, she would pay. They would all pay. Food would be cut off for a couple of days and the hunger pains usually hurt more than the fists. So, it was decided that they would just pray their way through the beatings.

"Don't you be worrying about what's beyond that window," he stated. "Nothing but sinners and madness."

Billy timidly shook his head in agreement. They had learned to always agree. No matter what. For their safety and for the chance to see Mother.

He walked around the basement and inspected a few more things. They all sat still and held their breath.

"I'm going to work now, and I expect things to be in order when I get home," he announced finally and turned to walk back up the stairs. Kelly knew what that meant. The house would be spotless, like every day, and his supper would be waiting for him to return. No matter what the hour. She wanted desperately to tell him of Beth's fever, but she knew it would do no good. It would only anger him.

When they heard the upstairs door close, the lock bolt, and the loud truck leave the driveway, they quickly got dressed. Kelly went over to the window, moved the curtains aside again, and gave it a nudge. It slid open partially. She closed her eyes, let out a sigh of relief, and silently thanked God. Another day had passed, and he hadn't noticed the broken lock on the basement window.

CHAPTER 3

The bells jingled loudly as the door swung open when Sheriff Brady entered and scanned the diner. Everything looked the same as usual. The *Talls*, as everybody referred to the couple due to their exceptional height, sat at their usual corner table, sipping tea, and eating English muffins. Chuck, the town eccentric, sat at his usual counter stool, mumbling to himself about the price of a cup of coffee. And against the main window sat the table of six men the waitresses referred to as the *coffee clutch*, talking over one another while trying to solve the world's problems.

Brady strolled over and as usual, there was one empty chair waiting for him. He pulled the chair out, rubbed his balding head and sighed loudly when he sat, as if any form of exertion was exhausting to his overweight frame.

Flora, the sixty-year-old waitress who had been working there since high school, promptly went over with a cup of coffee and a small, square, pillow. She set the coffee down in front of him and handed him the pillow. He propped the pillow behind his back. Plagued with back problems for a good twenty years now, he, and pretty much everybody in town, knew that if he wasn't careful, it could render him immobile for days. How he was able to pass a physical endurance test, nobody knew. Or cared, for that matter.

"Morning, George," she said with a smile. "Got your usual in."

"Thanks, Flora," he replied and winked at her.

"They keep raisin' taxes, ain't nobody gonna wanna stay in this town," Enos, the loudest of the coffee clutch, said with authority.

"It's been years since we raised taxes," retorted Frank. "I've been the mayor for, oh…ten years now. Last time we raised them was probably the last time you opened your wallet to let those moths out!"

Enos huffed as the others erupted with laughter.

Brady smirked as he sat and listened to the banter. It was like this every morning. They all knew everything and would argue their points while they ate their breakfast and sipped their coffee.

"What was all the racket on Main Street last night?" Arnold, the oldest of the group, asked Brady.

He chuckled. "Oh, just a couple kids got caught sneaking out after curfew. Nothing I had to do. Old man Rolands took care of his boy and the rest of 'em."

They all laughed. "Oh, I'm sure he did," Frank added. "That boy got a lotta balls thinking he can pull one over on his old man like that. I'm guessing they all got a well-deserved ass whoopin'!"

Brady sat and enjoyed the gossip. It was a quiet town for the most part and not a lot usually went on for him to contend with. They would sit and carry on like this, for around an hour, and then go their separate ways. They were all retired, except for Brady, who was counting down to his final year, two weeks, and twenty-one days.

Flora came back to the table to bring Brady his eggs, bacon, toast, and an oversized helping of fried potatoes when suddenly there was a loud squeal of tires followed by the bang of metal outside the diner. Brady struggled to his feet and stood to look out the window.

"Oh, Christ," he mumbled, as he looked out at the truck and car that appeared to be in a minor collision at the only traffic light in town.

'I'll be back!" he yelled to Flora as he headed toward the door with the coffee clutch following close at his heels.

When he reached the traffic light, he immediately recognized the rusty, blue pickup owned by Charlie Johnson. A middle-aged couple and a young man were getting out of the station wagon, in obvious distress.

"Everybody okay?" Brady asked, as he scanned the fender bender. The wagon didn't seem to look touched at all, but Johnson's pickup had a slight dent in the driver's side door that collectively matched the rest of the vehicle's exterior.

"The light was green!" Johnson grumbled, loudly, as he squeezed his large frame out of the truck.

"Alright, Charlie, take it easy," Brady said and held his hand up to silence him.

The man from the station wagon finally spoke. "Sir, I believe it was red." He reached in his pocket and pulled out his wallet. "Here's my insurance card," he said and handed it to Brady. "And my license."

Brady took the license and read his name out loud. "Pete Owens. Chicago?" he said and looked at him quizzically.

"Yes, Sheriff. We just moved here from Chicago."

"Probably should have stayed there!" Charlie spat. "And learned how to drive."

"Okay," Brady said impatiently and looked at Charlie. "Doesn't look like much damage. You can probably pop that out yourself."

Charlie glared at Brady but then quickly dropped his eyes when Brady sternly returned the glare.

Brady looked back at Pete and then at Nancy and Tommy and smiled. "Well, welcome to Oxville. Where abouts you gonna live?"

"We bought the Bradshaw house," Pete answered. He looked at Charle who immediately gave him a look of disgust.

"Well, I ain't got time to stand here and watch you pamper these people," Charlie growled and while still eyeing Pete, continued, "Just make sure you stay outta my way if you know what's good for ya."

He crawled back in his pickup, backed up, and squealed away. Pete stood stunned. *No insurance exchange? No ticket? The pick-up was clearly at fault. And was that last comment a threat?*

"Don't mind him," Brady assured him. "His bark is worse than his bite. He's mostly harmless. Pull your car into the diner lot and I'll buy you a cup of coffee."

Pete looked at Nancy, who still appeared a bit shaky. But after a moment she nodded her head yes and, in a few minutes, they were seated in the diner.

After the much-needed break filled with coffee, omelets, and a friendly interrogation from the coffee clutch, the Owens got back in their car and continued to their destination. They drove for about three miles before finally turning off onto a narrow, quiet, country road that was surrounded by endless trees and hills.

"Drive fast, Dad," Tommy chided, "In case there are cannibals waiting to ambush us!"

"Don't worry, Tommy," Pete laughed, "I'm sure if they saw the way you ate that omelet, they'd run the other way! And besides," he continued, "I think we've had enough action in this car for one day."

They drove a couple more miles down the road and then finally arrived at their destination.

"Here we are!" Pete announced as he veered the car into the long, maple tree-lined driveway.

"Are you sure this isn't Cinderella's castle?" Nancy asked in awe when the house came into view.

Pete smiled. "Oh, it's much better. It's ours."

Tommy's heart was racing as well. It truly was magnificent looking. It reminded him of the house he'd always admired in a painting that hung in the library back in Chicago. The large, two-story house was white with black shutters and featured a wide, white, wrap-around porch. An oversized flower garden, with an array of colorful rose bushes and bouquets of brilliant perennials, nestled in front of it. Off to the left and back a bit, stood a big red barn with a white gable-roof that peaked at a rooster weathervane. And behind the barn there was a wide-ranging horse pasture encased with a white paddock fence.

The huge yard had miles of trees scattered throughout. But one in particular caught his attention. Standing tall in front of the house, outshining all the others, stood the tree which he had always dreamed of. From one of its towering limbs, hung a tire gently swinging from a rope. Excitement filled him. As a small boy, he had always wanted a tire swing. But it was a little impossible while living in the twelve-story apartment complex they had just left behind. And although he was a *much* bigger boy now, he couldn't wait to give it a try. He smiled to himself. Maybe he could get used to this place.

As they got out of the car, Tommy looked at his dad, who stood proudly watching his mother squeal in delight at all her surroundings. Pete had come earlier in the Spring to find this home, but his description did not do it justice. That much was certain.

Tommy's thoughts were interrupted by the sound of a deep voice clearing on the porch. He looked over to find a tall, older man with a head full of white hair, wearing a white t-shirt and a pair of denim overalls rising from a rocking chair. None of them had even noticed him there. He stepped off the porch and smiled a wide, toothless grin.

"Hello, Mr. Owens!" he blurted out and extended his hand.

"Harry!" Pete exclaimed and rushed over to shake his hand. "Nancy! Tommy! Come meet Mr. Bradshaw. This is the man who sold us this magnificent home. He's lived here for eighty-two years!"

Tommy looked at the man, surprised. He certainly didn't look like an eighty-two-year-old man.

"My goodness, Mr. Bradshaw," Nancy said with sincerity. "If the air here keeps you looking this young, I am staying forever!"

"Harry, please. And you don't have to flatter me. The house is yours. I just wanted to welcome you all before I left."

Just then a green pickup truck pulled into the driveway. It was an antique model and seemingly in mint condition. The driver, an older man wearing a black checkered beanie, tooted the horn, gave a wave, but stayed inside the vehicle.

"Looks like my taxi's here," Harry chuckled, and waved back to the driver. "Be there in a minute, Jake!"

Nancy looked around the yard again.

"I know it's none of my business, but why in the world would you want to leave this beautiful place after all these years?"

He gave a long sigh and glanced around before answering. "My daughter insisted I move down to Florida with her and her family. I told her to move back in here with me, but my son-in-law has some fancy law firm down there." He looked down for a moment and thought hard before continuing. "I can't seem to remember his name right now." He shrugged and looked back up. "Anyway, she's always fussin' over me about something. Says I need someone to take care of me and I shouldn't be alone." Then he winked. "I think she just wants me down there for my good cookin!" They all laughed and then he turned and looked sadly at the house. "Yes, sir," he continued. "Was born in that house. Got married in that house and raised all six kids in that house. When my Maggie died, I tried to keep the kids here, but they wanted out of this town. Wanted to move into the big, fancy cities. Guess they didn't know a good thing when they had it."

He cleared his throat and then looked back at them.

"Well, I won't keep you folks any longer. Gotta catch me a plane for the first time in my life. Did I tell ya my son-in-law was a fancy lawyer?"

"No, that's wonderful," Pete lied. "Are you sure you can't stay awhile and fill us in a bit on the Oxville gossip?"

"I'd love to, Mr. Owens, but I don't have the time. You'll find that things are pretty quiet around her. But thanks anyway. And good luck with everything. I left my number in the kitchen in case you have any questions."

He shook Pete's hand, squeezed Nancy's and then slapped Tommy on the back as he leaned into whisper to him, "I think you'll like it here. There's a bunch of pretty dames in town. I've been checkin' 'em out myself. Sadly, for them, I'm leaving."

Tommy laughed with him as he turned away to climb back up the porch steps to grab his suitcase and head back down toward the green truck.

"You all take care, now!" he turned and shouted to them.

Nancy and Pete happily waved goodbye. But Tommy did not. He felt a sudden sense of sadness for Mr. Bradshaw. The once vibrant man oddly seemed to age when he glanced back at the house one last time as the truck was pulling away.

Once they made their way inside the house, Tommy felt like he had taken a step back in time. Although tastefully decorated, the interior had the feel of a solid 1800's home. The detailed ornamental features declared that it had more than likely been built with an abundance of time and care. They were speechless as they began their tour that began in the kitchen. Except for Nancy. She excitedly rambled on about everything she planned to do in that kitchen. At the top of the list was canning the endless list of vegetables that she would be growing. Pete and Tommy continuously smiled knowingly to one another. It had been a long time since they had seen her this delighted.

From there they continued to explore the rest of the house. Once they made their way to the second floor, Pete and Nancy, of course, claimed the master bedroom and then let Tommy choose from the other five. He chose the next largest, which captured the view of the backyard. And reasoning that because it faced east, he was certain that it would invite the perfect sunrise. Something the towering buildings in Chicago had forever denied him.

A horn blew, which sent them all scrambling back downstairs to discover the last moving truck arriving with perfect timing. Most of their furniture had already been delivered, but this truck was loaded with the necessities that they had used up until the last minute before the move. And towed behind it was Nancy's 1969 white Chevy Camaro. It was her *baby* and was treated so. She kept it clean and immaculate, and any miles put on were heavily monitored.

They spent the rest of the day setting up their beds and putting furniture in order for as long as they could before exhaustion set in. Pete ran into town for a few groceries and a large pepperoni pizza, which they eagerly devoured when he returned. And it wasn't long after that that they exchanged goodnights, looking forward to a much-needed sleep after a long day.

As Tommy turned off his bedroom light, he smelled an unfamiliar kind of air blowing gently through his window. It was fresh and pure. He breathed in deep to capture the scent that he knew could never be captured in a candle or a spray. An aroma that only nature could provide. He got out of bed and pushed the curtains aside. The moon was full, and it spread a soft gentle glow across the countryside, giving the earth a kind of serenity that he had never sensed before. He peacefully crawled back into bed and was fast asleep in a matter of minutes.

CHAPTER 4

Two weeks had gone by, and the Owens family was still busy cutting through the chaos of moving to a new town. Pete was at his new office in the next town over adjusting to his new position as the plant engineering manager for the modular home facility that branched off from its corporate office in Chicago. Nancy was busy rearranging miscellaneous items in the house to fit her taste.

Tommy walked downstairs from his bedroom and headed toward the refrigerator for his morning glass of orange juice.

"Hi, Mom," he said when she followed him into the kitchen to greet him. "Can I use your car today? I thought I better take care of some things at school."

She pursed her lips in jest. "Sure, honey. Would you like me to go along?"

"You can if you'd like but I shouldn't be too long. They should already have most of what they need. I just wanted to grab my schedule."

"Well, then you may as well go by yourself. I can go shopping when you get back. Make sure you park far away from other cars."

"And keep my distance on the road," he continued, mockingly irritated. "And if necessary, I shall use my body to shield the car from potential harm." He knew the drill. Reassurance that he will treat her *baby* as if his life depended on it.

She laughed. "And, *most importantly*, keep my baby boy safe."

He laughed. "I'm a big boy, Mom."

"You're still my little boy," she said and stood on her tippy toes to kiss him on the cheek.

"Oh, Mom. You'll be saying that when I'm fifty."

"You're right. Now get out of here before I put you to work."

"I'm going!" he shouted in mock annoyance and grabbed the keys from the countertop.

***

When he reached the school and walked up to the front doors to let himself in, it felt strange. And small. The school secretary was a pleasant older woman wearing red glasses that humorously matched her hair. She made him feel welcome immediately. While looking through his prior school transcript, she raised her eyes with approval.

"You should do fine here, Thomas," she said, and smiled when they were finished. "You should have probably come in a little sooner, but that's alright. We'll get your schedule all set up. I will need your parents' signatures on a few things though, so if you could, have one of them stop sometime before next week." She looked back at his papers. "You play soccer. And quite well, I see. MVP for your junior year? Impressive. I'm sure the Oxville Oxens could use you on the team. Oh, and one other thing. The bus on your route will probably come around…" she paused and fumbled through a few papers. "Here we are. About six-thirty."

"Thank you," he replied, "But I plan on driving to school."

Knowing Nancy would not let him have full reign with the Camaro, Pete had hunted down and found him a cheap, practical truck for him to get around in. Unfortunately, it would not be available for another week.

"Okey, doke," she replied, a little surprised. "Most of the kids around here aren't able to drive to school, so there isn't much of an assigned parking lot for students. But I'm sure you can park along with the faculty. And please don't hesitate to ask for any help while you're here. Finding classrooms and such."

"Where I'm from, one grade is the size of your school," he laughed. "I *hope* I will be fine."

She laughed with him, shook his hand, and wished him luck.

When he left the office, he walked around the school for a while and looked into some of the windows of the classrooms. He was suddenly starting to feel a little nervous and anxious about attending this new school next week. Maybe all he needed was a familiar voice from Chicago to calm his nerves. He headed to the car thinking about Tanya. He had tried calling her a few times already with no success. But today, he thought, it might just be his lucky day. He started the car and let the top drop down on the Camaro, allowing the warm summer sun to fill the car.

While driving back through town to head home, he was forced to stop at the traffic light in town. As he sat there waiting for the light to turn green, he looked over and noticed a group of kids standing on the corner checking out the Camaro. The girls who stood with the group smiled with obvious approval. He gave them all a friendly wave, but only the girls returned the gesture. The boys, on the other hand, began to shout offensive comments.

"Look at the rich boy!" one of the boys shouted. "Guessin' he's lost!"

"Yeah!" shouted another, "The beauty salon is two streets over!"

He wasn't letting the banter bother him. His father had always taught him to never give a jealous person your power. And that's what it was. Jealousy. But when he heard someone shout, "Probably Mommy's car! Same car was parked in my driveway last night!" he caved.

He cursed them in his mind, and when the light turned green, he held the brake and slowly pressed the accelerator to get it revving and then quickly released the brake while holding down the accelerator. The rear wheels spun and sent out a shrill, high-pitched sound while creating a thick black smoke that billowed up and drifted toward them. The car shot off quickly and he smiled to himself when he looked in his rear-view mirror to see the guys in the group flailing their arms and shouting.

But the smile didn't last long. A few seconds later, when he glanced back into the mirror, he unfortunately spotted red and blue flashing lights speeding up on him. He let out a deep sigh, slowed, and reluctantly pulled over to the side of the road.

***

"Owens," Sheriff Brady said calmly as he leaned in to look in the car and then take a step back to observe the outside.

"Sixty-seven?" he asked.

"Sixty-nine," Tommy answered, regretting having to correct him.

"Hmm..." Brady said and shook his head in admiration, "Yours?"

"Mom's," Tommy replied, awkwardly.

Brady nodded his head again. "She teach you how to burn rubber like that?"

"No, sir," Tommy answered and put his head down.

"I figured not," he continued. "Guessing she'd be a little disappointed to know about it."

"Yes, sir," Tommy answered again.

"Well," Brady said and straightened his posture as he glanced around. "Probably no point in telling her then. As long as it doesn't happen again."

"It won't, Sir," Tommy promised.

Brady nodded, tapped the top of the door, and left to get back in his cruiser.

It *was* his lucky day, Tommy decided as he once again headed toward home, making sure to heed the speed limit with extra caution.

***

In good spirits he dialed Tanya's number when he got home and when he finally heard her voice on the other end of the line after all these days, his heart raced.

"Hello?" an out of breath, high-pitched voice answered.

"Tanya!" he exclaimed. "I'm so glad you finally answered. You're a hard girl to get a hold of. I've missed you so much!"

"Tommy?"

"Who else?" He laughed. "How are you doing?"

"Alright. I've been busy trying to get ready for school."

"Yeah, me too. It's so good to hear your voice."

"Well, I can't talk long right now. I'm getting ready to go shopping with Cathy. *Again.* You know how I love clothes."

"Yes, I know," he replied, feeling his heart sink a little.

"Have you made many friends?" she asked.

"Not really. Might be easier once school starts."

"Yeah, prolly," she answered with a distracted voice and then repeated, "Sorry, Tommy. I really can't talk too long."

"Yeah, okay. Sounds like you got a hot date," he joked.

She didn't laugh.

"Tanya, you know I'm joking."

"What? Sorry, Cathy's here. She's waiting for me. She thinks I can talk to two people at once."

He heard chatter and giggles in the background.

"I can call another time," he said, reluctantly.

"Yeah, that would be better. I really have to get going before this girl drives me crazy."

More giggles.

22

"Okay," he answered, "I love you."

"What? I really have to go, Tommy," she replied with a hint of annoyance.

"Okay. Talk to you later. Have fun."

He hung up the phone and felt the world collapse around him. The coldness in her voice hurt and confused him. He couldn't help but feel that he would have felt more of a connection if he had dialed a wrong number and talked to a complete stranger.

His mother came into the room and immediately sensed his agony.

"Everything okay, Tommy? Do you want to talk?"

"No, I'm fine," he said quietly. "I think I just need a walk."

He went outside and picked up a broken branch from the ground and tore off the arms to make himself a walking stick. He looked around wondering where he wanted to walk before finally heading towards the pasture. He crawled under the fence and kept on walking towards the woods. He thought about Tanya and all his friends back in Chicago. No one there probably missed him, he concluded as he jabbed the stick into the ground with each step. It hurt. All of it. He still had his parents, he knew, and maybe he could make some new friends here, but only one person mattered at the moment. He wanted *Tanya* to care about him.

He reached the other end of the pasture and crawled under the back section of the fence. Reaching the woods, he aimlessly wandered on. The thick trees seemed to go on for miles and he wondered if he might lose his direction and get lost. But he didn't care.

Eventually he came upon a babbling creek. The sound immediately soothed him. He bent to pick up a couple small, flat, rocks to skip across the water, but after many attempts, couldn't get past a second skip. While sarcastically snickering at his lack of talent at this game, he was stopped short by the sound of laughter somewhere in the distance. He paused and listened hard. There it was again. Giggling coming from down the creek aways. *Who in the world would be out here,* he wondered and decided to go investigate.

After a short stroll, he came upon a girl that looked close to his age, with a younger girl and boy next to her, in the creek. Their skin was covered in mud, and they were trudging through the water, barefooted. He watched for a while, observing them, and found it amusing that the mud was only on their exposed skin and not on their clothing. They were laughing and kicking water at one another. They looked so at ease and happy that it contagiously poured over onto him and made him smile. He watched them for a while longer, allowing all the sour feelings to seep from his body.

"Hello!" he finally shouted and proceeded toward them until he reached the edge of the creek.

They gasped and moved close together with wide stares upon their faces.

"Do you live around here?" he asked and smiled to help with their uneasiness.

None of them spoke. They just stared at him with frightened eyes.

"I'm Tommy," he said and held out his hand to the oldest girl as he approached.

She didn't take his hand. Instead, she looked at the other two children and firmly said, "Let's go." They both frowned openly and put their heads down, keeping a wide eye on this new stranger.

"Wait!" Tommy said, confused. "I'm not gonna hurt you. I'm new around here. Where do you live?"

"If this is your land, we are sorry. Come on kids, we need to go," she said nervously.

"No!" he rambled, hurriedly, "I mean I don't even know if this is my land. It doesn't matter."

The girl took the two smaller children by the hand and briskly led them out of the water. Without looking back, she quickly headed down the creek's bank in the opposite direction. Tommy rushed to catch up to her and took her by the arm to stop her and gently spin her around. She immediately recoiled away from him.

"I'm not going to hurt you," he pleaded. She stared hard at his hand on her arm until he finally let go. The smaller children continued to curiously stare at him.

"What is your name?" he asked the younger girl and bent slightly to meet her height.

"I'm Beth!" she answered excitedly.

The older girl glared hard at her.

"I'm Billy!" the young boy added eagerly.

"You mean like Bronco Billy?" Tommy teased.

"What's that?" the boy asked, ignoring the older girl's glare.

"What?!" Tommy teasingly shouted and then proceeded to do his best imitation of a cowboy riding an imaginary horse and waving an imaginary hat in the air while hooting and hollering as the two younger children erupted into laughter.

"You're silly!" the younger girl squealed.

He could see the older girl fighting hard to contain a smile. "Come on you two," she commanded as her eyes nervously darted about.

Tommy tried again. "How come you got that mud on your face? Are you trying to scare the squirrels?"

Again, they burst into laughter. "No, Silly!" Beth chimed in. "It's to keep the sun from burning our skin so…"

"Beth! That's enough!" the older girl scolded, angrily.

"It's okay," Tommy said. He quickly bent down to scoop a wad of mud from the creek bank and rubbed it on both his ears. "I didn't hear a thing. I think I got something in my ears!"

This time the older girl laughed aloud. The sound enlivened him. He smiled at her and tried again to extend his hand to her. "I'm Tommy. Nice to meet you. And your name is?"

This time she slowly took it and shyly smiled back. "I'm Kelly."

He could see the beautiful smile behind her muddied face, but it was her blue eyes that really caught his attention. They sparkled like none he had seen before.

"Well, Kelly, you have a very pretty smile," he said. Billy and Beth both giggled loudly.

"What's so funny about that?" he asked the children. "You think that's funny? Maybe you'll think this is funny too!" he teasingly shouted and leaned down to tickle them both in the ribs. They squealed with laughter and darted out of his reach before running off to chase one another. But it was short lived, as the younger girl erupted into a coughing fit and went to sit down on a rock to catch her breath.

"Be careful!" Kelly yelled to them with the smile still on her face.

"Do you come here often?" he asked Kelly, and then immediately regretted it. It sounded too much like a corny pick-up line.

"We try. The kids really like it here," she responded, indifferent to his question. "And Beth's not feeling well. Bringing her outside helps. I can tell."

"It is nice," he agreed, glancing around. "I'm from Chicago, so you could imagine the change of scenery it is for me."

She stared at him blankly.

"So, how old are you?" he asked, changing the subject.

"Um...sixteen?"

"Great, maybe I'll see you in school?"

"No," she said quickly. "I don't go to...that school."

Tommy laughed. "Which school?"

"It's just a different school," she said, slightly annoyed. "We mostly learn at home." He decided not to pry any further. The last thing he wanted to do was to come across as some kind of creeper.

They continued to talk for quite some time, with Tommy doing the majority of it. He was pleasantly surprised how at ease she made him feel. She listened to him chatter about his life in Chicago with such fascination that he found it hard to stop until she suddenly looked up to the sky and interrupted him by announcing to the children that it was time to go. The children and Tommy simultaneously groaned loudly. Kelly laughed out loud again.

"It was nice to meet you," Tommy finally said, disappointed that their encounter was ending. "It feels good to make a new friend. Maybe I will see you here again?"

"It was nice to meet you too, Tommy," she said with a smile and then quickly hurried the children off into the woods.

***

Tommy thought about Kelly and her siblings for the next two days. On the third day he decided to go back to the creek. He looked for them unsuccessfully and decided that maybe he had scared them away for good. It didn't seem normal that he should have felt so much sadness over this, but he did.

He headed back to the house and decided that he could catch Tanya at a better time. Maybe he was over-thinking their conversation the other day. Maybe she *was* busy. And knowing Cathy, she probably was being a pain.

"No, she's out," came Tanya's mother's voice over the phone.

He hung up the phone with disappointment and turned to see his mother standing in the doorway watching him, with concern in her eyes.

"Hey," she said, trying to lighten his mood." You probably haven't talked to your buddy, Frank, in a while. Why don't you give him a call? He always knows how to spark you up."

She was right. Tommy had been friends with Frank since they were in second grade, and he had always had a way of making Tommy laugh. Most of the time it ended up with Frank at the principal's office or grounded, but in the end, they would have a memory to laugh about.

He grabbed the phone again and dialed.

"Yo! Tom! How's the little farmer boy?" Frank answered cheerfully.

"Oh, great. Just got done milkin' the cows and fetchin" the eggs," Tommy replied.

"That a boy! How many farmers' daughters you had up in that hayloft?"

"Oh, I'm not telling you, you dog. Last thing I want is for you coming around messing things up."

"And I thought we were friends!" Frank laughed.

Becoming serious, Tommy hesitantly asked, "Have you seen Tanya around at all?"

Frank was quiet for a moment. "Nope. Not too much."

"Frank, she lives next door to you. Give it to me straight."

"Look, Tom, we've been friends for a long time. I'm just gonna say don't be sitting home waiting around too much."

Tommy let out a grunt. "So, what's his name?"

Frank hesitated again and then reluctantly answered "I don't know. He's a freshman at the university. Walks like he has a stick up his ass."

Tommy was quiet.

"Listen Tom, I know you don't want to hear this but she ain't worth it. Besides, you really can't expect to have a relationship with this much distance between you. Get out there and meet some of those country girls. You know you're the stud, man!"

"Yeah, yeah, yeah." he replied, trying to hide the sadness that had consumed him.

"Listen, I gotta run. Nice to hear from you. Keep me posted on your life there. I wanna know all the juicy shit! Maybe I can plan a trip out sometime."

"Yeah, that would be great. And Frank, thanks for putting it out there."

"You'll get nothing less from me brother. We'll talk soon."

Tommy hung up the phone and sighed. His mother was right. The call was just what he needed. Even though the truth felt like a punch to the gut, it was what he needed to hear. He had already suspected this truth and now he could work on settling his thoughts.

But his thoughts went back to Kelly. She was quite a mystery for sure. There were so many things he wanted to know about her. She certainly seemed like a sweet girl. And he was certain that if her face hadn't been covered in mud, she would have looked far better than Tanya. No frills needed. *Stop!* He scolded himself. *You are done with girls!*

CHAPTER 5

As soon as she heard the truck drive away, Kelly rushed upstairs with Billy and Beth to make their usual pot of oatmeal. They ate quickly and then Kelly sent them back downstairs to get dressed while she cleaned up the kitchen.

After she was finished, she went downstairs to get dressed as well. She went into the tiny bathroom that was no larger than a broom closet and proceeded to brush her hair. The bathroom consisted of one small toilet that was full of rusty water and a five-gallon bucket of cold water that was placed on the floor. The bucket, that she filled every morning from the basement sink, allowed them to sponge themselves daily with a little bit of privacy.

They were not allowed to use the bathroom upstairs. Father would know. A strand of hair, a tiny pool of water, or anything out of the norm would alert him. Even a square of toilet paper missing would set him off. She silently thanked God again for the creek that he did not know about for it allowed them to occasionally submerge into a full bath of natural spring water for at least six months out of the year.

While washing her face, she suddenly wished that she had the mirror that she'd done so long without. Father had taken it from her. Vanity was the devil; he had reminded her over and over. She felt her face with her fingertips. Tommy had said she had a pretty smile, she remembered, and then smiled. He had also said that they were friends and that made her feel good inside. She had never had a friend, except for Billy and Beth, but it felt different. She didn't understand these feelings that she was feeling, but she knew she liked it, and she couldn't wait to see him again.

Billy and Beth were dressed and playing a game of "I Spy" that Kelly had taught them when she came out of the bathroom. She decided to steal a few more minutes to herself. She walked back to the far side of the basement and slid aside the large piece of paneling that lay against the wall. Behind it there hid a thin door about her height with a small hole halfway down where a knob once existed. She opened the door with a hard tug and squeezed in the space that was about the size of four closets. It was their little hiding spot where they could hide the things they had collected over the years that they did not want Father to find. He would surely take these things away if he knew they brought pleasure to them. Inside were a few toys the children had found through the years outside, by the creek and in the woods, along with a few crayons that they could draw pictures with on the paper that Kelly would take from the mail pile.

And then there were Kelly's special things. She bent down and pulled out her greatest treasure. It was the calendar that she took once a year from the mail pile that sat on the kitchen table upstairs, unsorted, sometimes for weeks. She took a crayon and marked off another day. She would often take other things of value from the pile in the hopes that he would never miss them. But the calendar, by far, was the most valuable thing to her. Besides the pretty pictures it usually displayed, it gave her a sense of time. She knew she was six years old when they had come to this house, and it wasn't long after that that Billy was born. Beth was maybe two, she figured. And regrettably, it was the year that her mother had left. She was not happy. Father had told her. We were too much for her. So, the babies became Kelly's responsibility until the day it was decided that they were good children. Good enough to make Mother happy again.

She remembered her birthday being sometime in the fall. It was right after the start of school, when the leaves began to change, and the air would begin to get cooler. A memory of the last birthday she could remember entered her mind.

"*Happy Birthday, to you…Happy Birthday to you…*" Mother and two other children had sung to her. She could not remember the other children's names, but she remembered them singing to her at the top of their lungs until it was time to blow the six candles out.

"*Make a wish!*" Mother had said, joyfully.

She couldn't remember the wish, nor if she was able to blow all the candles out in one breath. She could only remember that the fun had stopped suddenly when Father had come home. He was shouting at Mother, and the children had left the house in tears. And she never saw them again.

She couldn't remember Beth's birthdate at all, but Billy she knew, was born around Christmas time. Mother had always made sure that Kelly and Beth had a cake and would somehow manage to give them something special. So, one day they sat down around the calendar, and they each picked a day to celebrate their birthday from year to year. Of course, it would have to be done in secret so that Father did not find out. They would draw each other a special picture and Kelly would somehow manage to sneak a special treat for them on their day from Father's pantry upstairs. There would be no point in asking him for anything extra. He constantly reminded them that they didn't appreciate what they already had.

She sighed and reached further into the hiding spot for the neat bundle of letters. She ran her hand over them slowly. They were all letters from Mother. She couldn't really read them but thought she could at least figure a few words out. Father would read them to her to remind her what was at stake. They always said the same things. They commanded the children to behave, obey their father, and to never sin. She would someday return when she was sure that the children were finally good children. The letters seemed longer than she thought Father was reading, so she was left to imagine what the rest of the words would say. She was sure that they read that her mother did, in fact, love them very much and missed them. And that she was so happy that Kelly was taking care of the smaller children the best that she could.

Of course, he would crumple up the letters and throw them in the garbage can when he was done reading them, knowing fully well how much they meant to her. But the following days, when he was away, she would secretly retrieve them, smooth out the wrinkles, and hide them away in this special hiding spot.

Kelly did not know what else was beyond the creek and the woods outside, but she did know that when Mother finally returned, things would be better. She just knew it. She gently put the letters back in their designated spot and closed her eyes. She thought of how very kind Mother was. Even kinder than her first-grade teacher. The only teacher that she remembered. Miss Stawback. Even though her time spent in that class was short lived, she missed that teacher very much. She missed the kids in that class. But mostly she missed her mother's big hugs right before she climbed the school bus steps.

She often told Billy and Beth stories about the life she could remember. Their eyes would light up. They too loved this mother that they did not remember, and they were sure she would one day save them from the man that lived upstairs. The man they called Father.

So, in the meantime, she would continue to be careful around Father so that she did not ruin things. She did not want him to tell

Mother what terrible children they were, and she definitely did not want to scare her away any longer than they probably already had.

CHAPTER 6

On the first day of school, Tommy was able to drive his new truck. Well, it wasn't exactly new. In fact, it was fifteen years old, with a few rust spots to offset the red color and some duct tape to cover the tears in the seats. But it was new to him, and he was pretty happy to finally have a set of wheels to call his own. He had never had to ride a bus to school and wasn't keen on experiencing it. He had always either lived within walking distance or belonged to a carpool.

When he walked into his first classroom, he felt about two inches tall when everybody openly stared at this *new kid in town*. Some whispered to each other, while others just openly made curious comments. They stared at his clothes and his shoes, which inevitably screamed Chicago. He made a mental note to perhaps shop for some flannel in the near future to blend in a little better. He glanced around the classroom for an empty desk. He could easily pick out the social status of the students. He could tell who the athletes were, who were the bookworms, and who were the loners. He chose a desk with the loners. It seemed fitting.

His first day of classes seemed like a lifetime, but he had made it through. As he was walking to his truck to head home, he came upon a group of students standing around it, checking it out.

"I think he's cute," he heard one of the girls say to another as he approached.

"Compared to what?' snorted a tall, dark-haired boy in a tattered baseball cap that faced backwards, standing next to her, smoking a cigarette. "My bulldog?"

Tommy immediately noticed the large scar on his forehead and a few on his arms just below his rolled-up flannel sleeves. *No doubt, battle wounds.* From what? He didn't care to find out on this particular day. He watched him as he took the cigarette out of his mouth, snubbed the ash out on the bottom of his work boot, and tossed the butt into the back of Tommy's truck.

"So, you're the new kid in town?" The tall kid asked with a crooked grin and broadened his shoulders.

Tommy looked at him for a moment and then scanned the group of boys who stood behind him like a pack of dogs waiting for a command.

"I asked you a question," the tall kid spat. "Cat got your tongue? Or maybe they don't teach you real manners in those big city schools?"

Tommy knew this was far from a genuine welcome wagon, so he reached in his pants pocket for his keys. But before he could unlock his truck door, the tall kid leaned against it, blocking the way.

"Excuse me," Tommy said, sternly, avoiding eye contact.

"Whoa! He does talk!" the tall kid retorted and looked around at the group for approval. On cue, they erupted in laughter.

"*Please* move," Tommy said, this time looking him directly in the eye.

"Ya wanna make me?"

"Alright, Dan, knock it off," interrupted the girl who had made the first comment.

He hesitated and then slowly moved away from the door while still eyeing Tommy.

"Yeah, I can knock it off for now. Just make sure you know your place around here. Or I'll have to show you."

"I'm sure you will," Tommy replied, annoyed, and then unlocked his truck door, climbed in and slammed the door shut. It wasn't until he started the engine that the crowd began to slither off, with Dan leading the way. Tommy instantly noticed that Dan walked with a slight limp. There was no doubt that he probably had to, more than once, *show someone their place*. They slowly headed off in the direction of the buses that were lined up along the curb of the school driveway. All except for one of the boys. He waited until the group was out of ear shot and then tapped on the driver's side window. Tommy waited a moment and then finally rolled the window down and looked at him. The boy scratched his curly, strawberry blond hair and grinned.

"Hey, listen," he said, with sincerity, "Don't let that shit bother you. He didn't like what his girl said about you is all. He thinks he's gotta be a tough guy. His father probably knocked a few too many rocks loose in his head. Just want you to know we're not all assholes here. Most. But not all." He stopped and held his hand out. "Anyway, welcome abroad."

Tommy grinned and reached out to shake his hand. "Thanks, man."

"Name's Riley. You're Tom, I know," he said and grinned again. "*Everybody* knows. Let me know if you need help. Anytime."

Tommy nodded, put the truck into gear after Riley took a step back and drove off.

***

When he got home, Nancy excitedly asked, "How was your first day of school?"

"Fine," he stated flatly, not wanting to talk about his day. He tossed his book bag on the sofa and turned to head back out the door.

"Where are you going already?"

"For a walk," he snapped.

"Are you alright?"

He let out a long breath and softened his composer before turning to her to lean down and kiss her on the cheek. "I'm fine Mom. Just need some air."

He walked out and headed towards the woods, feeling bad for losing patience with his mother. She was the last person who deserved the wrath of his mood. And no doubt, probably sick with worry that something was drastically wrong.

When he made it to the woods, he walked until he found the creek again and sat down on a large rock that was nestled on its edge. He picked up a handful of rocks and tossed them in anger, one by one, into the creek, wondering what the second day of school would bring. One thing was for sure; he wasn't going to put up with Dan's *loose rocks*. He never looked for a fight, but if there was one thing his father had taught him, it was to stick up for himself. And he wouldn't care if the whole school hated him. He grunted. *They probably already did anyway.*

"You look so sad," came a soft voice from behind him, shaking him from his thoughts.

He turned to see Kelly. She had mud on her face again and was wearing a ragged gray dress that seemed two sizes too large for her slender frame. His face lit up. Even in that condition, she was still a sight for sore eyes.

"Kelly," he said with a smile and stood up. "I thought you disappeared from the face of the earth."

"How come?"

35

"Because I've been down here a few times, and you were nowhere to be found."

"I mean how come you look so sad?" she asked with concern.

He sighed. "It's not important. At least not anymore. I'm happy to see you though. Where is Billy and Beth?"

Happy that he had remembered their names and asked about them, she replied, "They're playing down the creek aways. Well, Billy is. Beth's just watching him. Her head is warm again today and she's kind of sleepy."

"Oh, that stinks," he said and took her hand and led her to the rock to sit with him.

"So, I *do* want to know," she said sincerely, "Why did you look so sad?"

"Well, it doesn't seem like a real big deal now, but it has to do with school today."

He bent down to pick up a stick and began to tell her about his day and how he had been treated by the other students, while aimlessly drawing circles in the dirt. She listened attentively to every word without interrupting. When he was finished, he looked at her to find her eyes wide with concern. This made him chuckle. "Really, it's not *that* big of a deal."

"It sure is a big deal," she said as a tear formed in her eye.

He quickly took her hand. "Hey, Kelly, look. No bruises."

She looked away, put her head down, and quietly said, "It *is* a big deal when people are mean." She turned back to him and asked desperately, "What makes them that way, Tommy?"

He shrugged his shoulders and shook his head with a frown. "I don't know. Bad experiences, maybe. Issues they can't resolve, I suppose. They can make you ugly or teach you empathy."

She looked at him confused and then frowned. "I'm not sure what you mean, but I wish everybody would be nice. And have *armpit...*"

"Empathy," he finished for her and chuckled.

Her childish innocence made him smile. He stared at her for a minute and then suddenly laughed out loud. She looked at him curiously.

"I'm sorry," he said, still laughing, "But it gets kind of hard to take you too seriously with all that mud on your face."

She laughed with him. "I look bad, huh?"

"Nah, just dirty. Why do you have it on anyway?"

"To keep the sun off my skin," she replied. "I don't like it to get red."

"Okay? A little sun on your skin isn't that bad. Besides, couldn't you use sunscreen?"

"Maybe," she answered, confused, and embarrassed at the same time.

"I'm sorry. I shouldn't pry like that. I can be pretty stupid sometimes."

"No, you're not," she said with a hint of anger in her voice. "I think you are really smart."

Before he could tease her about the comment, Beth and Billy came running up behind them singing "The Farmer in the Dell", another song that Kelly had taught them. Her face lit up as she stood to address them.

"Just a little while longer and we need to head back," she warned.

"So soon?" Tommy asked. "Can I walk you guys' home today?"

"No!" Kelly said quickly. "Father doesn't want strangers at the house."

"But we're friends now, aren't we?"

Kelly smiled at that. "Yes, I think we are. But you still cannot come."

"Fine. I surrender. As long as you promise to come back tomorrow?"

"Okay. Only if there is no rain. And it will be at this time." She pointed to a large tree with the sun just above the tallest branch. He laughed. But she did not. Surely, she had to have been teasing him. *Was she really using the sun as a clock?*

He decided to leave it alone and instead continued with a chuckle, "Ok Cinderella. I wouldn't want you to change into…" he thought deeply for a moment, "I'd sure like to know."

"A princess," Kelly cut in. "That's how the story goes. I know that one."

He smiled again, amused. "You're already a princess."

She blushed and giggled and then stood up to find the children. She galloped over to them, grabbed their hands, and together they began to skip away.

"Bye Tommy!" they shouted to him over their shoulders as she led them off.

"Tomorrow!" He reminded her with a wide grin on his face and watched the three of them skip off into the woods.

CHAPTER 7

Kelly made sure the window was closed, and the curtain was exactly where it belonged. She ran upstairs to peel potatoes and cut beef up for the stew she was going to make. They had spent way more time in the woods than they should have and now she had to hurry.

"Billy, you dust and Beth, you sweep," she ordered. Neither complained. They knew the price of spending the entire day outside as well. Kelly was usually the only one permitted to leave the basement to go upstairs. And it was only to cook, clean, and then return to the basement with a scant serving of food for the three of them to share. God only knew what her father would do if he knew the younger kids were up there as well, but she had no choice but to sneak them up there to help her with chores if they stayed away too long. And she had no way of knowing when he would return home. So, she would have to keep reheating the dinner until the sound of his truck pulled into the driveway. There were some days when he did not return until long into the night. And those nights were the worst. He reeked and stumbled and slurred his words with more anger than usual.

Once she had made the mistake of falling asleep at the kitchen table because he had not come home until almost daylight. He had accused her of allowing Billy and Beth time alone to sin. And it was Billy who paid for her mistake with his tiny body.

No matter how much she cleaned, it didn't seem to make the house any more appealing. It was much smaller than the one she remembered as a little girl. Most of the walls were covered in peeling paint or wallpaper. There was one couch with a few tears in the fabric and a reclining chair that did not match. Or recline. The kitchen had a stove, a small refrigerator, and a table that only had one chair.

As soon as the supper was cooked and the chores were done, she heard the truck pull into the drive. Cursing her luck, she realized he had come home earlier than usual. She quickly rushed the children downstairs with her without a chance to gather food for the night.

They all gathered on one of the mattresses and whispered to each other.

"Are we gonna eat?" Billy asked, worried.

Kelly thought for a moment. "Maybe he'll leave again. Then we can go back upstairs."

They all sat in silence and prayed. An hour went by, and Beth finally spoke up. "I'm hungry Kelly."

"I know," she said and stood up.

She paced the floor thinking of what to do. Beth, especially, needed to eat. She still wasn't feeling good, and her cough seemed to have gotten worse. She cursed him in her mind. For all he knew, these children didn't even eat. And he probably didn't care. She heard her own stomach growl, and she looked back at the children. She had not heard his footsteps upstairs for a while, so she decided to take a daring chance.

"Listen, I'm gonna sneak upstairs. Maybe he's sleeping. You guys have to be really quiet."

"You better not, Kelly. It's not a good idea, "Billy whispered.

"It'll be alright. Just keep extra quiet."

She quietly went up the stairs with every step keeping pace with each exploding heartbeat in her chest. She opened the door at the top of the stairs as softly as she could, and panic shot through her when it let out a sharp creak. She caught her breath and listened hard. Relief swept over her when she heard the loud snoring coming from the back bedroom.

She tip-toed into the kitchen and glanced around the corner to make sure the coast was clear. The stew still sat on the stove, untouched. She dared not to disturb it at this point in fear that it might get noticed. Moving to the cupboard, she opened the door and stood on her tippy toes to reach for the box of saltines that she immediately spotted and began to slide it toward her. The box pushed against a jar of sugar causing it to slide out to the edge of the cupboard and tumble downward. In a split second she was able to catch it with her other hand. She closed her eyes for a moment, sweating, and thanked her luck. She placed the sugar back in its spot and looked again in the cupboard until she saw an almost empty jar of peanut butter. She grabbed it and held it firmly in her hand. She took a breath and slowly turned around and her heart stopped.

There he stood in his angry mask of fury. She froze.

"Whatcha got there?" he asked, powerfully.

"I was hungry," she quietly said, after a moment.

"Think I can afford to buy snacking food?"

"I didn't eat supper," she answered timidly.

"What?!" he thundered.

She hesitated and then said slightly louder. "I said I didn't eat supper."

He reached out and snatched the crackers and peanut butter from her hands and slammed them on the kitchen table. "Sit and eat, then!" he commanded.

Shaking, she sat down in the chair and stared at the crackers. "Couldn't...couldn't the kids have some too?" she asked quietly.

There was a long silence and then he let out a loud, vile laugh.

"I knew it! This was their idea! Sending you up here to do their dirty work."

"No, Sir. I was hungry too," she stammered.

"Then eat," he stated, finalizing the conversation.

She slowly took a cracker out of the box and began to nibble on it. Guilt welled up inside her knowing that the kids were hungry downstairs. He glared at her until she put her head down and gently laid the cracker on the table.

"What, my food not good enough for ya?'

"I guess I'm not really that hungry."

"Then get back down where you belong!" he roared and pounded both fists on the table causing the box of crackers to bounce up and fall to the floor.

"You appreciate nothing!"

As she scrambled to her feet, the chair flipped backwards and crashed into the floor. She stumbled forward and fell on her hands and knees. Without hesitation, she quickly crawled to the basement door and scurried down the steps and did not stop until she reached the bottom. He slammed the door hard behind her.

Her eyes had become accustomed to adjusting to the darkness quickly over the years, so she was able to run directly to the children who were still huddled on the mattress. She hugged them tightly, still shaking. She then took three deep breaths to try and calm herself before finally speaking.

"Tomorrow morning we'll eat extra," she promised.

"But I'm hungry now," Beth whined.

"Can't you see that she tried!" Billy scolded her.

Kelly put her finger on her lips to quiet them. Beth began to sob softly but before Kelly could reach out to comfort her, Billy had his arms around her.

"I'm sorry," he said softly.

"I know," she said and sniffled. "I know." She took a deep quivering breath and looked at Kelly. "Can you tell us more stories about Mother?"

Kelly smiled as the tenseness slowly left her body. "Of course." She gathered the children close and together they laid down and curled up upon the mattress.

"Um…let's see," she began, "She would make me pancakes for breakfast. And sometimes for supper! They're round and fluffy and very yummy. With sweet syrup that spreads all over them. And she would make snowman pancakes at Christmas."

"Do we have to talk about food?" Beth asked, groggily.

The three of them laughed softly.

"I hope Mother makes us snowman pancakes," Billy said. She could sense his smile, even in the darkness.

"Was Christmas fun?" Beth asked.

"Yes. Mother made it very fun. She said it was Jesus' birthday and should be celebrated. She would put a *real* tree in the house, and I would help her hang stuff on it to make it pretty. And we would sing. And bake cookies."

"I can't wait to have Christmas with Mother," Beth said and yawned.

Kelly continued to tell the children stories so that they would not think about their hunger until they both fell asleep. She then snuggled even closer to them, draped her arm over them, and continued to think about Mother. She would never tell the children about the sad stories. The ones where Father had kicked the tree down in anger, causing many of the pretty ornaments to shatter on the floor. Or when he would yell at Mother for hours on the other side of Kelly's closed bedroom door, breaking things until she could hear her crying.

Her mind flashed back to one memory in particular. She was awakened by the sounds of a slamming door and the baby crying in a distant room. And when she walked out of her bedroom and into the kitchen, she found her mother crumpled on the kitchen floor.

"*Momma?*" she called softly.

Her mother lay there silently. She carefully walked over and bent down next to her and moved the hair aside that covered her face. Mother continued to lay motionless, and her swollen eyes stared blankly at the floor. There were bruises on her neck and dried blood stains on her nightgown.

"Momma?" she had repeated more desperately and reached out to cradle her face in her tiny hands. Her mother slowly looked up at her.

"Kelly…" she muttered, *"Please go get Beth."*

She did as she was told and left to pick up the crying baby from her crib and gently rocked her, as she had seen her mother do so many times, until the crying subsided. She carried the baby, whose tiny body felt very heavy in her little arms and whose little feet bounced off her knees, into the kitchen and looked down at her mother again for more guidance. Her mother slowly rose into a seating position, wincing in pain with each movement, and sat up. She looked at Kelly and managed to smile. *She would always manage to smile.*

"Can you get her a bottle for me, honey?" she asked weakly.

Kelly hesitated. *"Momma, should I go ask Cecile for help?"*

Cecile was the older, heavy woman that lived next door. She had a hard time getting around, blaming it on her bad knees. Kelly liked her. She always had a batch of fresh baked cookies waiting for her whenever she was allowed to play outside. And Mother liked her as well. She could tell. The two of them would chat for hours outside during the summer, laughing and smiling the whole time.

But Father did not like her. She had no problem speaking her mind to him and she most certainly was not afraid of him. And he knew this. He accused her of filling Mother's head with garbage and that was why she was not allowed in their home. So, Mother learned to keep their visits a secret.

"No," her mother managed. *"I don't need Cecile. I'll be okay. Just give me a minute."*

And she eventually was okay. After weeks of healing, life went on as normal. The only normal that Kelly knew.

Those were the sad stories she chose to never share with the children. Those were the memories that haunted her the most.

CHAPTER 8

The second day of school was a little easier for Tommy. His classmates didn't seem to stare as much and they pretty much left him alone. He paid attention to the morning announcements and decided he would sign up for the soccer team after school. Soccer was one of his biggest passions and he wasn't about to let this big change in his life take that from him.

Later that day, as he was sitting in the cafeteria eating his lunch alone, the girl from the previous day suddenly plopped down beside him and set her tray next to his. She took a fork and moved the food around on her plate with a look of disgust before dropping it back on the tray. She turned, looked boldly at Tommy, and smiled. He looked around nervously. "Are you sure you wanna be sitting here?"

She flirtatiously giggled and flipped her long, wavy, auburn, hair off her shoulders.

"Why wouldn't I?"

"Um...Dan?"

She rolled her eyes and tsked. "Dan doesn't own me." She held out her hand. "I'm Catrina."

He noticed her fingernails immediately. They were meticulously manicured with a loud, red color. Tanya flashed through his mind, and he couldn't help but notice an uncomfortable resemblance. Reluctantly, he shook her hand loosely and replied, "Tommy."

"Yeah, I know. Everybody pretty much knows everything about everyone here." She began to use her red nailed fingers to count and list all the facts that she did know.

"I know you moved here from Chicago. I know you bought the old Bradshaw farm. I know your father is the new plant manager for *Feros*. I know you're one of the few kids here that drive to school. Not the hot car I saw you in a week ago, but no biggie. What I don't know is, if you have a girlfriend."

Kelly, oddly, flashed through his mind. He wanted so much to say yes, and that she was the kindest, prettiest, girl who had more class in her unpolished little pinky than anybody in this entire school. But she wasn't. In fact, he wasn't sure what she was. A friend for sure. But there was so much more he needed to know about her.

"Well?" Catrina asked, interrupting his thoughts.

"What?"

"Do you *have* a girlfriend?"

He reluctantly nodded his head no and looked around. "Speaking of, where is *your* wonderful boyfriend?"

She snorted. "Well, if you were to ask Dan, he would say he's my boyfriend. But if you were to ask a few choice girls around here, they might beg to differ." She sighed and slowly shook her head. "He doesn't think I know. But like I said, everybody knows *everything* about everyone."

"That stinks," Tommy said sincerely, relating to the feeling.

She smiled and gazed seductively into his eyes. "Yeah, but someday he needs to learn that life can go both ways. A lot of guys would kill to go out with me. Maybe I should see what else I'm missing. Don't you?"

He became uncomfortable with the conversation. A lot of guys might have been flattered by her bold flirtation, but he was not. Sure, she was pretty enough. But the kind of pretty that probably took some time to pull off. And she certainly was not worth the trouble of Dan. But most of all, she wasn't *Kelly*.

"Am I interrupting something?" came the familiar, unwelcoming voice from behind them.

They both turned to see Dan standing there looking perturbed with his arms crossed in an irritated manner.

"Just a friendly conversation, Dan," Catrina answered, annoyed.

"Well, I think it's over. Let's go, Catrina," he said, staring hard at Tommy.

She rolled her eyes and got up to take him by the arm to lead him away. Tommy could hear them arguing in the distance. He started to feel sorry for her, but that ended quickly when he heard her proclaim that it was *he* who had invited her to sit. So, without question, he decided to stay clear of that girl. Everything about her spelled trouble.

***

When school finally let out, he headed to the gymnasium to sign up for the soccer team. He scanned the group of boys as he entered and immediately spotted Dan, who needless to say, gave him a look of contempt. Trying hard not to feel intimidated, he ignored him and walked to the back of the line.

"Hey!" Riley said when he turned to see Tommy. "Glad to see you're joining the team! We could use some new talent. *Any* talent, really. You do have talent, don't you?" he asked, skeptically and grinned.

"Maybe," Tommy answered. "What position do you play?"

"Forward," he answered. "How about you?"

"Same. At least I try," he replied, humbly.

"No worries, I'll carry ya," Riley assured him and smirked.

When the group finished signing their names, they walked over to sit in the first two rows of the bleachers and waited for Coach Reynolds to give his talk. To Tommy's surprise, he overheard a few of the kids discussing that this was Coach's fortieth year with the Oxville soccer team. As he approached them dressed in a gray sweatsuit, Tommy couldn't help but notice how tall and lean Coach was. Except for a slightly protruding belly that clearly hinted that he might enjoy a cold beer or two, he was in pretty good shape for his age.

Coach scanned the list on his clipboard as he looked up at each student while scratching his disheveled, graying hair. When he came to Tommy's name, he announced it out loud and looked around inquisitively. Tommy raised his hand. Coach raised his eyebrows and observed him for a moment.

"So, you're the superstar?" he finally asked with an impressed tone.

Riley, who had taken a spot next to Tommy, glanced at him with surprise, but Tommy didn't respond. Although he maintained the record at Castle High School back in Chicago for the most goals scored in one season, he wasn't particularly fond of the attention it was currently bringing him. Especially with Dan glaring at him from the bottom end bleacher.

"Can't wait to see your style," Coach continued, before turning his attention back to the entire group to announce practice schedules.

Riley nudged him with his knee. "Hey," he said quietly. "You must be good. Coach isn't usually this easily impressed. In fact, you'll find out that he's pretty much brutal. He once had us all line up and walk past him right after he farted. Wanted us to know what he thought of us. *We stink.*"

Tommy let out a burst of laughter and then quickly put his head down.

"Something funny?" Coach asked and looked in their direction.

"No, sir, Coach. You have our full attention," Riley answered with an exaggerated politeness that mimicked the voice of Eddie Haskell from Leave It to Beaver as he nudged Tommy with his knee again. Tommy kept his head down in an attempt to hide his grin. When he looked back up, Coach was still staring at him.

"I didn't think so," Coach said sternly and then looked back down at his clipboard.

Just then a group of girls wearing tight cotton shorts and t-shirts of assorted colors began to randomly enter the gym and gather in the opposite corner.

"Cheerleaders," Riley whispered to Tommy under his breath. "We usually don't give 'em much to cheer about, but they're nice to look at anyway."

A few of the girls made a point to walk closer to the guys' bleachers on their way through to get a closer look at them. Leading the pack was Catrina. She mumbled something under her breath, and they all glanced up to look at Tommy.

"Looks like you're quite the novelty," Riley quietly snickered to him.

Tommy made a half-hearted grin and then looked over to see Dan standing up and glaring at him.

"Sit down, Rolands," Coach commanded him. "I'm not done yet."

Dan slowly sat back down with a scowl on his face but kept his eyes glued to Tommy.

"Looks like the girls aren't the only ones that can't keep their eyes off ya," Riley humorously said, under his breath.

"He's not my type," Tommy whispered back, sardonically. "Lacks a brain."

This time it was Riley who burst out laughing. Coach looked up at them again but, as if on cue, Riley's face quickly took on a serious, attentive expression. Once again, Tommy had to bow his head to contain a chuckle.

When the meeting finally ended, Tommy went back to his locker to grab a few books before heading home. He was feeling pretty good about the soccer season starting, especially with Riley on the team. But that changed rather quickly when he got to his truck to discover that his back left tire was flat. He cursed under his breath and went around the back to retrieve his spare. He heard a scoff and turned to see Dan and Catrina walking past him, arm in arm. Dan mockingly laughed at him and then mumbled the comment that he should watch out for those pesky nails. He had figured Dan might have had something to do with it but wasn't about to give him the satisfaction of acknowledgement.

***

While driving home, he got the sudden urge to drive into town and stop at the local gift shop. As usual, Kelly was on his mind, and he wanted to get her something special. As soon as he walked in the door, he immediately spotted the perfect gift. One long stemmed, freshly cut, yellow rose surrounded by baby's breath, sat in a milky white vase that had a yellow ribbon tied around it. Simple, yet beautiful. Perfect, like her. It didn't take long to find the perfect card either. It simply thanked the receiver for being a special friend. He couldn't have written it better himself, he decided, and smiled in the hopes that it would bring a big smile to her face as well.

He paid for his purchase and headed out to get back in his truck when he suddenly stopped short. He couldn't give Kelly something special without bringing something for the kids. They were kind of growing on him too and he rather enjoyed seeing them excited. But mostly, he knew how much it would mean to Kelly.

He went back into the store and after searching through the merchandise for a bit, found a box of assorted chocolate candies. He opened the box to make sure a few of his favorites were in there as well. They were good kids and probably would be more than happy to share it with this *big kid*. He bought them and finally headed home.

***

Later that afternoon when Tommy reached the creek, Kelly and the kids were already there. He held the gifts behind his back and walked up to them.

"Hi!" he exclaimed and smiled widely.

They all took a step toward him, curious as to what he was hiding.

49

He looked at Billy and Beth and said, "I have something for you if you know the magic word."

They looked at him confused.

"Go ahead and guess!"

They both shrugged.

Tommy exaggerated a long sigh. "Okay. The magic word is *Tommy is the greatest!*"

"Tommy is the greatest!" Billy yelled out, no longer able to hold his curiosity.

"What a wise observation!" Tommy shouted, while Kelly laughed. He took the candy out from behind his back and handed it to him. Billy stared at it, not sure what to do with it.

"*Words*," Beth mumbled.

"What?" Tommy asked and looked at her confused.

"Magic *words*. Those are words, not word."

Tommy smiled and nodded. "Got it, Little Miss Professor. Now go ahead and open it. It's for both of you. But save me the four pieces in the corners."

They slowly opened the box and stared at the chocolate pieces and then looked up at Kelly in wonder. She knew what they were and immediately became emotional. She remembered her mother giving her candy. It was on rare occasions, but she could remember the joy it brought to her. A tiny tear escaped her eye.

She nodded in approval to them to go ahead and taste the candy. They each took a piece out and slowly chewed on it. Both their faces lit up. They smiled widely with chocolate smeared teeth and looked up at Tommy in bewilderment.

"Go ahead, have another! They're yours!"

Then he looked at Kelly and wiped the tear from her cheek. "It's just candy, Kelly."

She looked at him. "Oh, it's more than just candy, Tommy. You are the greatest."

"You said the magic words," he said sweetly, exaggerating the *s* and pulled his other hand out from behind his back and handed her the rose attached to the card. By then, the tears were streaming down her face.

"Kelly," he said and took her face in his hands and wiped the tears from her cheeks with his thumbs. "It's supposed to make you happy."

"Oh, Tommy. It makes me very happy." She smelled the rose. "It's lovely."

Billy and Beth ran off with their candy and sat upon a large rock by the creek to begin devouring each piece.

"Why?" Kelly asked.

Tommy shrugged. "Because I like you. Now go ahead and read your card."

She took the card out of the envelope carefully and slowly brushed her hand over the cover. It was a picture of a cluster of daisies. Just like the ones in her dreams. She looked up at him and smiled.

"Thank you so much, Tommy. It's wonderful."

He laughed. "Aren't you even going to read it?"

She opened it slowly, glanced at it, and then put her head down in shame. Her hands were trembling, and another tear was forming.

"Hey, Kelly. What's the matter? You didn't even read…" he began but stopped mid-sentence as realization struck him. He let out a sigh before softly asking, "You can't read, can you?"

She continued to look down. He gently lifted her chin up and looked sympathetically into her eyes. "It's okay. I didn't know. I'm sorry."

"I know," she whispered. "How could you know I was stupid?"

He stepped back abruptly. "You're not stupid!!" he insisted, his eyes wide with anger. And then he softened his voice. "That's why I'm so surprised. I *know* you're not stupid."

He sighed again and looked around. "What about school?"

Her silence told him there was no school.

After some thought he continued. "Maybe I can help you. I can bring you some books and teach you?"

Her eyes lit up. "You would do that for me?"

"It would be my pleasure," he assured her.

"And the children? Can they learn too?" she asked,

He smiled and shook his head yes.

"But," she continued cautiously, "It will have to be down here. And at the same time."

"That's fine," he answered excitedly, looking forward to spending more time with her.

They sat down together, and Kelly flooded him with a thousand questions about his school and what happened during his day and how many friends he has when suddenly they heard a painful scream. They jumped to their feet and ran towards the kids. There they found Billy lying in the creek holding his leg and sobbing in pain. The box of candy was upside down and floating gently down the creek. Beth was crying as she tried unsuccessfully to help him up.

Instinctively, Tommy jumped in and scooped Billy up in his arms and out of the creek. His calf was cut open and there was blood oozing from it. Tommy laid him on dry ground and quickly took off his shirt to wrap it around the wound.

"We need to get him home! You lead the way," he ordered Kelly, after picking Billy back up into his arms.

She stood wide-eyed and speechless, unbudging.

"Kelly!" he shouted sternly, hoping to snap her from her fright. After no response, he hurriedly began to carry Billy off and through the woods towards his house with Beth close at his heels.

Kelly caught up with them and began to plead with Tommy, "Please just let me take him home!"

With deaf ears, he continued to carry Billy off with both the girls trailing behind him.

As they reached his house, Nancy was just coming out of the front door and onto the porch. "What in the world?" she asked in a panic.

"Billy cut his leg, Mom," Tommy said loudly and rushed him to her. "He needs help!"

Nancy looked at the leg, gasped softly and asked him if they shouldn't take him to the hospital instead.

"No!" Kelly cried. Nancy turned to see this unkept, innocent-looking young girl with a world of terror in her eyes that undoubtedly convinced her that this was not an option.

Nancy quickly led Tommy, with Billy in his arms, into the house and into the bathroom where she proceeded to carefully clean the wound and then bandage it. When she was finished, she looked at Billy and asked if he felt okay. He didn't answer her. He only stared at her, as Beth did, with wide eyes.

"Well," Nancy said as she looked at Kelly, "I don't think he needs stitches, but make sure you tell your parents right away." Kelly shook her head that she would. Nancy then turned to Tommy. "Come see me in the kitchen, please."

When they left the bathroom, Beth looked at Kelly and asked, "Is she Mother, Kelly?" Kelly gently took her in her arms and replied softly, "No. She is Tommy's mother. But ours is just as pretty and smart. I promise."

In the kitchen, Nancy asked Tommy who the children were. He proceeded to explain how he had met them in the woods by the creek and how he had been spending a lot of time with them.

"Something's not right, Mom. And I feel this incredible need to help them, but I don't know how. Kelly won't open up much to me about her family, or her life."

"They look so unattended, Tommy. And so terrified. And undernourished," she said, sadly. "And the little girl…she looks very sickly."

"I guess she's not been feeling well. They're wonderful kids, though, Mom," he said with a smile. "And Kelly…well, she's kind of special to me."

The conversation was interrupted when the children came into the kitchen. Billy had a slight limp but otherwise seemed to be faring well. Beth was coughing again but trying very hard to contain it.

"We have to go now," Kelly said to Nancy. "Thank you so much for your help."

"Why don't you stay for dinner?" Nancy quickly asked.

"Oh, no." Kelly stated. "We have to get home before dark."

"It's almost done now," Nancy pleaded. "And there's still a couple hours more before dark."

"Please Kelly?" Beth cut in.

Kelly looked nervously out the window and thought for a moment.

"Please?" Billy added.

Kelly sighed with defeat and smiled. "Okay. Just a little while longer."

And then they all smiled. But no smile was bigger than Tommy's.

While Nancy continued preparations for dinner, Tommy took the three on a tour of the house. Kelly paused to softly touch everything they passed, including the furniture, the bedspreads, and even the curtains. The children were in awe and surprisingly speechless for a change. But it was the television that piqued their interest the most. Tommy had turned it on for a moment to show them the surround sound feature. They stood and stared at the pictures that bounced across the screen with amazement. Kelly had to forcefully take them by the hands to pull them away from the screen and into the next room.

"This is what a castle is?" Kelly asked with wonderment when the tour was finally through.

Tommy laughed. "Well, I wouldn't go that far but it sure is bigger than the apartment we had in Chicago." He took her hand and led her into the dining room with the children following behind.

During dinner, Nancy unsuccessfully tried to learn the children's history. Kelly was as vague as possible with her answers while Billy and Beth kept their mouths full and silent as they ravished their fried chicken and mashed potatoes. Kelly sternly glanced at them from time to time to get them to slow down. Nancy caught this and laughed.

"Tommy used to be the same way at their age," she assured her. "Always in a hurry to get outside and play."

If only that was the reason, Kelly thought. Nancy looked at Billy. "Seems you are doing okay. You were very brave for such a young man. How old are you?" He looked at Kelly in the hope that she would handle the question. But Kelly, once again, evaded it and rose to gather empty plates from the table.

"I'll do that," Nancy said quickly and stood up. "You're a guest."

Kelly was more than confused by this but obeyed Nancy and put the dishes down. This was *her* job. *Always.* Beth then stood up and burst into yet another coughing fit. Only this time it was so violent that she gagged and threw up her dinner all over the floor. Nancy instinctively rushed to her side to comfort her while ordering Tommy to get some paper towels. She gently coaxed her back into her chair and reached down to touch her forehead.

"This child is burning up," Nancy said with alarm. She looked at Kelly in a panic. "Has she seen a doctor?"

"She will," Kelly lied.

"And she should be home resting."

"I know," Kelly replied with embarrassment. "We are going now."

"Is she taking anything for this?"

Kelly's silence told Nancy that she was not.

"Tommy, go to the medicine cabinet and grab the acetaminophen."

He quickly ran upstairs and returned with the medicine bottle. Then he went to the kitchen sink to quickly fill a glass with water, returned to the table, and handed it to Beth. Nancy opened the bottle and handed her a dose. Beth just stared at it, not sure what to do.

"It's okay," Nancy coaxed her. "Just swallow it. It'll make you feel better."

Beth looked to Kelly for guidance. Being that it did not take Kelly long to fully trust Tommy's mother, she nodded to Beth with approval for her to take the pill.

"Has she been sick for a while?" Nancy asked Kelly.

"No," Kelly lied, wanting to downplay Beth's illness to avoid having to discuss any of their present living conditions.

"Okay. I'm sure your parents know better, but make sure she gets plenty of fluids and rest. And here," she continued as she handed Kelly the bottle of pills. "You can keep these. She can have one every four hours if the fever comes back. And Billy could use it too if his leg starts to hurt too much."

"Thank you," she said, with deep sincerity and then looked at the children. "We have to go now." They both sighed openly, which made Nancy laugh out loud. "Now that doesn't sound like a popular idea. But know that you are always welcome here. Here, wait!" she said and rushed back in the kitchen to return with three oranges. "You forgot dessert!"

The children took the oranges and smiled at her and Tommy could tell that they had already won her heart.

"I'll drive you home," Tommy said to Kelly.

She remembered the rose and the pretty card that she had left at the creek in their haste to get Billy help. The rose would have to be tossed before she returned to the house, she decided. There was no way that the fragrant scent would not be noticed in that musty basement. But the pretty card? *That* she could hide.

"No," Kelly stated, "We will walk."

"Then I will walk you," Tommy replied, with defeat.

"To the creek," she finished.

He sighed and shook his head, "To the creek."

As they all stood to head out the door, Nancy quickly cut in, "Tommy, hang on. I need to talk to you."

He looked at her and then at Kelly and said, "I'll meet you guys outside."

Once they left, Nancy looked at Tommy and sighed.

"There is no doctor, is there?"

"I don't know, Mom," he replied. Surely Kelly would have mentioned a doctor if Beth had gone to one. "I'm guessing no."

She tsked. "I don't want to step on her parents' toes or get them in any trouble, but something has to be done for that child."

He looked at her worried. If she pushed things, it could get ugly. Social Services could get involved and take the kids away and he might never see them again. But he knew Nancy wouldn't just sit back and not try to help Beth either. He thought for a minute and then asked, "Do you still keep in touch with your friend, Anna? The doctor?"

"Yes, but what good is that going to do if she's in Chicago?"

"Well," Tommy hesitated, and then continued, "What if she could prescribe something over the phone to the local Pharmacy?"

Nancy was taken aback for a moment and then raised her eyebrows. "That's asking a lot. But I could probably talk to her. Find out Beth's symptoms besides the fever and cough. I suppose it's worth the try."

"Thanks, Mom," he said and hugged her tightly before walking out the door to join Kelly and the children.

CHAPTER 9

It was the first game of the season and Tommy sat on the bench in a black and gold uniform feeling anxious. Soccer had always come so naturally to him, but this game was different. It was the first time he would be playing for a new school, and he knew all eyes would be upon him. Being a small town, it was pretty much known what each player had to bring to the table already. But not him. His practice sessions had convinced Coach that the MVP status he carried with him from Chicago was indeed accurate. His ability to handle the ball with such precise skill had landed him a starting position, much to Dan's dismay.

"It's not fair that he should start," Dan had argued. "It's not fair to the guys who have been playing since our freshman year."

"I'm the coach. I'll make the decisions," he had responded, finalizing the subject.

So, when they lined up for kick-off and the whistle blew, it became obvious rather quickly that Dan was going to make sure that Tommy did not get the chance to touch the ball, even if it cost them the game. And it seemed most of Dan's cronies were on board with this decision as well.

At the half while Coach lectured the team on how they weren't scoring because they were all probably afraid of getting a run in their pantyhose or dropping their lipstick, Riley leaned into whisper to Tommy, "Dude, I'm trying to get you the ball. They ain't making it easy."

"I know. You're good," Tommy replied, already knowing in his mind that he was done playing Dan's game. It was time to turn the heat up and show Oxville what *he* brought to the table.

Coach finished by yelling, "Put your diapers back on and get out there and do something!" And with that they rose and ran back out on the field to start the second half.

With ten minutes left in the half, the score was 4 - 0, with the Oxens losing. Riley was working as hard as he could to score, but the opposing goalie was just too good. And any attempt to get the ball to Tommy was stopped by *both* teams. Tommy's stubborn and competitive nature finally went into overdrive, and he decided he would have to take desperate measures. He ran up and stole the ball from one of his own teammates and quickly dribbled it up the field, maneuvering in and out of each player on the field, including his own teammates, until he reached the goal. Without missing a beat, he swung his foot as if he were aiming for the goal but instead curled his left foot behind him and used it to slam into the ball. This tactic threw the goalie off and as he leaped to one side of the net, the ball swiftly rolled past him and into the opposite side of the net, creating their first goal.

Riley ran to him and lifted him high in the air as the crowd cheered loudly. His other teammates leaped for joy as well. But not Dan. He purposely turned and impatiently headed back to the center line. The goal seemed to inspire a few of Dan's cronies, because they changed their tune and began to pass Tommy the ball for the remainder of the half. He scored three more goals in what seemed like a matter of minutes. But it wasn't enough. With just a few seconds left, the opposing team scored one last goal, winning the game 5 - 4.

Tommy dropped his head in disappointment and slowly began to trudge off the field.

"Woo Hoo!" Riley shouted as he ran up behind him to give him a hearty side hug. Tommy looked up to see everybody in the stands standing and clapping. *They seemed happy with the loss.* He looked at Riley with confusion. Riley burst out laughing and excitedly explained, "We made the scoreboard! We hardly *ever* make the scoreboard!" The humor of the situation made him smile as well as he headed to get in line with his team to low five the opposing team in sportsmanship. When they were finished, Coach happily slapped Tommy on the back.

"We got ourselves a ringer!" he explained, happily. "See you guys on Wednesday!"

Coach had an odd practice schedule. They practiced every other day and never the day after a game. It was no wonder they never made the scoreboard, Tommy mused. But he didn't care. He was having fun in spite of the team's attitude, and it only meant more time to meet up with Kelly.

He walked to the bench, grabbed his gym bag, and scanned the bleachers to find his parents. In the twelve years that he had been playing the sport; they had never missed a game. As he was looking,

Catrina purposely came into view. She was wearing her Oxville Oxens cheerleading outfit and smiling confidently at him as she approached.

"Nice moves," she said, with a seductive grin. "Kinda figured you'd have that quality."

He half-heartedly nodded to her and then looked around. And just as he figured, Dan was making his way over.

"Catrina! Let's go!" Dan commanded her. She rolled her eyes, turned to him, and placed a hand on his arm when he reached her side. He abruptly knocked it away all the while refusing to look at Tommy. Then he turned away from her and proceeded off in a huff. She quickly caught up to him and after a couple attempts to take his hand, he roughly grabbed her hand and briskly led her off. Tommy watched for a moment as they crossed the field to leave. He didn't know whether to feel sorry for her or not. It seemed she brought on some of her own troubles, *and* she always had the choice to break up with him. Either way, he concluded, it still gave Dan no excuse to treat her the way he did.

"Friends of yours?" he heard Nancy happily ask from behind him.

He turned to see his parents standing there, beaming with pride.

"Sure," he said, wryly, not wanting to cause her any undue worry.

"You looked good, Son," Pete added and patted him on the back. "Looks like your coach could use some coaching of his own, though. But at least you got to show 'em your worth in the end."

"Yeah," Tommy said and smiled at him.

"Tom!" Riley yelled as he walked past them. "The team's going for pizza at Dinos! You coming?"

"Gonna pass!" he answered and waved to him. He didn't know if Dan was going or not, but he *did* know that he wasn't in the mood for any more drama today.

"You're sure?" Nancy asked, a little disappointed.

"I'm sure, Mom."

And with that they headed across the field and to the parking lot.

***

After school the following day, with a book in his hand and a ball at his feet, Tommy dribbled the soccer ball the entire distance to the

59

creek. His team may not be practicing every day, but that wasn't going to stop him.

Kelly and the kids were already there waiting for him. They looked curiously at the ball as he kicked his way to them.

"What's that?" Billy asked with excitement.

"It's a soccer ball. You've never seen one?"

Billy nodded his head no.

Surprised, he continued, "Well, I'm gonna show you how to play."

"Tommy," Kelly interrupted. "Aren't we having a reading lesson today?"

"We will," he answered her and grinned. "But I think we should start with recess today."

They looked at him confused. "What is recest?" Beth asked, only slightly mispronouncing the word.

"*Recess* is just as important as learning lessons," he explained. "It's down time. Time to play and feed your body's muscles. Like reading feeds your brain."

"We already play," Beth insisted.

"I know, but this is more of an organized play."

"I think I would like to have that kind of play!" Billy burst out.

Tommy laughed. "Okay! Let's go!"

He found a larger than normal opening in the woods and placed them each in a spot until they formed a big square and then proceeded to teach them how to pass the ball to each other. They did this for a while and since they seemed to be enjoying it so much, he took it a step farther. He grabbed some rocks and set up two makeshift goal areas. He took the ball and began to teach them the game of soccer. Eventually he split them into teams of two, with Beth on his team and Billy on Kelly's, so that they could begin to play the game.

He downplayed his skills tremendously to keep the three of them interested and to make sure they were having fun. Kelly and Billy caught on rather quickly, but Beth was having a hard time coordinating her feet. At one point she went to kick the ball out from Tommy's feet, even though he was on her team, and her little leg got tangled in his. It forced him to lose his balance and, to not hurt her, he purposefully fell to the ground. He grabbed his knee with his hands and rolled from side to side in make believe agony.

"That's a penalty!" he yelled.

"Yay!" Beth squealed. "I got a penalty!"

Tommy laughed loudly. That was a lesson for another day.

"You sure did," he smiled and rose to his feet.

They continued their play and at one point Kelly took control of the ball and dribbled it toward her goal. Tommy caught up to her and when he tried to cleverly steal the ball from her feet, she darted to the side and kicked hard, landing her foot smack in the middle of his shin. This caused him to yelp with pain and fall to the ground. Once again, he rolled from side to side in fake agony, but this time when he stopped, he laid flat and still with his eyes closed shut. In a panic, she quickly dropped to her knees by his side and shook his shoulders.

"Tommy!" she cried out. When he didn't respond she reached out to try and lift one of his eyelids.

"Ow!" he yelled, this time with sincerity, and popped his eyes open. She then opened her own eyes wide and glared at him. The look on her face caused him to roar with laughter. She pursed her lips in dismay and then gave him a gentle smack on the arm.

"Ow!" he yelled again and sat up to quickly pull her to the ground next to him. He rolled over and propped himself up beside her and began to relentlessly tickle her. She laughed so heartily that it almost looked like she was in pain.

"Stop!" she cried out with laughter. "My stomach hurts!"

He stopped and looked down at her with the smile still painted on his face. She looked up at him and was still smiling as well. Out of nowhere, a wave of admiration washed over him. The smile left his face and all he could do was stare intently into her eyes. Her beautiful blue eyes. The smile then left her face as well as she struggled with what was happening. The feelings building up inside her were confusing and she didn't understand what they meant. But the moment was short lived when Billy and Beth jumped on Tommy's back. They were laughing and trying to pull him back to the ground. He followed along with their playfulness and pretended to be much too weak to fight them off. Kelly quickly rose to her feet and straightened her dress. The fun had suddenly become strange, and she needed time to sort through these new feelings.

Tommy finished wrestling with the children and then stood up with a smile still on his face as he looked at Kelly. But his smile quickly diminished when he saw the look on her face. She seemed embarrassed or ashamed. He couldn't really tell.

"Hey," he said softly to her. "You okay?"

She nodded her head yes. "We should get going."

"No reading lesson today?" he asked, concerned.

"No," she quickly answered. "It's getting late. We can skip today."

"Awe!" Billy whined. "I want to play more soccer! This was the best day *ever*."

"We can do it again," Tommy assured him without taking his eyes off Kelly. She seemed out of sorts, and he had to guess, *or hope,* that maybe she too was beginning to feel something for him. The shy smile on her face when she turned to say goodbye as the three left to head back into the woods told him that they were still good. And that was all he needed to know.

CHAPTER 10

The big talk of the school was the homecoming dance. All the students were raving about how much fun it was going to be. Tommy had made a few friends by now and as they all sat around the lunch table eating the day's serving consisting of chicken nuggets and macaroni and cheese, they began to hound him on who he would be taking to the dance.

"Well, I'm not sure that I'm even going," Tommy said.

"Man, you have to go, Tom. You're the reason why we just didn't make the scoreboard but actually won some games!" Riley chimed. "It's a riot, I promise. And if it's a date you need, I'm sure you won't have any trouble in that department. I hear there's a few girls more than interested in you. Just say the word and I'll hook you right up!"

Tommy chuckled. "Well, I appreciate that, but the problem is that the girl I would *really* like to take probably won't be able to go."

"What?!" Riley jokingly exploded. "You holding out on us? Who is she? What girl's got a stud like you hooked?"

"Her name is Kelly…" he started and then laughed. "You know, I don't even know her last name. How's that for *hooked*?"

"Well, that sounds serious!" Riley chuckled. "What's she like? She good lookin'?"

Tommy smiled and shrugged. "She's kind of different. Great. But different. I can't explain it."

"Hmm…" Riley pondered, teasingly. "That doesn't tell us a whole lot. But if you change your mind, let me know. Rumor has it that Catrina is pretty hot for you." He laughed boisterously at his own statement.

"Yeah, so is her boyfriend," Tommy joked back. Everybody at the table joined in with the laughter. Dan's temper was no secret.

"She's definitely not worth the trouble," Tommy said, seriously.

Riley smiled, knowingly. "Yep, I guess you're hooked."

Tommy suddenly got charged. "Maybe you guys know her! Her name is Kelly. I'm guessing she lives on the road behind that big stretch of woods behind my house."

"You're guessing?" Riley laughed and then thought for a second. "This might be a small town, but I can't think of any Kelly without a last name. In fact, don't really know anybody on that road 'cept that miserable Johnson guy. And he lives alone. You need to ask a few more questions. Why doesn't she come to our school?"

He shrugged. "Not sure. Guessing she's homeschooled. And not very well at that," he snorted.

Riley burst out laughing. "I wouldn't repeat that to the parents!"

"No chance there," he assured him, slightly agitated and then stood up. "I'll catch you guys later. Want to get to the library before lunch period ends."

"Such a model student you are, Owens," Riley laughed.

Tommy smirked and then saluted them in jest before heading off to the library to get more books to take to Kelly and the kids.

***

Once at the creek, Tommy shared his day with Kelly like he always did, at her persistence, before beginning their reading lesson. When it was her turn, she happily shared the news that the pills that Tommy had brought her from the pharmacy did indeed help Beth and that her cough seemed to have gotten much better. He was pleased with the news and reached over to squeeze her hand with a smile. Their conversations had become the highlight of his days, and he knew he could easily spend the rest of his life sharing days like this with her. But knowing that their hours were limited, and he still had a pressing question that he wasn't sure how to bring up, he opened the book that he had brought to choose their next lesson. The children paid attention for a little while, but like usual, got bored and wanted to run and play. After they went through a few pages, he folded a piece of paper, placed it on the page that they were working on, closed the book and looked at her.

"Is something wrong?" Kelly asked, with concern. He hesitated nervously for a few minutes before finally speaking. "You know, there's this dance at school. It's coming up soon and is supposed to be a lot of fun."

Her face lit up. "How nice for you! I don't know a whole lot about dances, but I hope you have fun there!"

He laughed. "Well, it would be a lot more fun if I had a date."

She looked at him blankly.

He tried again. "So, what do you say?"

64

Again, she looked confused. "What do I say?"

"About going with me," he continued, slightly annoyed, "I want you to be my date for the dance."

"No," she stated flatly and to further dismiss the subject, she took the book from his hands, opened it back up to where he had marked it and pointed to a word. "Now how do you make the sound in this word again?"

Tommy didn't answer her. He just stared at her in disbelief.

"Tommy," she said again, "How do you pronounce the letters in this word again? Is it *ir* or *ar*?"

He suddenly seized the book from her hands and glared at the word in anger.

"It's *ar*. Like in *hard*! You know, like cold? Or down right rejectful?" He was now glaring angrily into her eyes.

She quickly recoiled and covered her face as if he were about to strike her. Immediately he realized his horrible mistake and softened his voice at once.

"Kelly, oh my god, I am so sorry." He wrapped his arms around her and held her tight to him to soothe her. And he continued to hold her until he could feel all the tenseness leave her body and then he pulled away to look into her eyes. "I'm so sorry. I would never hurt you."

She looked at him painfully but said nothing.

" What's happened to you?" he pleaded. "What is your life like to make you this way?"

She put her head down, not knowing how to answer this. She wanted to share everything with him but was ashamed. But mostly she was afraid. The consequences were much too dire.

After her long silence, he continued, "I like you so much. Do you not like me?"

She looked at him sadly. "Oh, Tommy, I do like you. So, so much. But it is very dangerous to go anywhere like that with you."

"Because of your father," he said with disgust.

"Yes," she answered quietly. "If you knew him, you would understand."

"Well, I'd like to meet him! I'm sorry, but I hate him already and I would sure like to give him a piece of my mind," he stated angrily.

"No!" Kelly said again, frightened. "You would ruin everything!"

"What do you mean?" he asked in desperation.

"Nothing" she said, quickly. She thought for a moment and then finally asked, "When is your dance?"

His face lit up with hope. "It's in two weeks. It starts at 6 o'clock. It's a Friday night!"

She sadly looked down again and slowly replied, "I have no good clothes. I can't come out at night. I have to care for the children…"

"I'll get you a dress!" Tommy interrupted.

"And we can watch us!" Billy chimed in, who was apparently listening in. "You can use the window!"

"Please go Kelly!" cried Beth. "You can tell us all about a dance when you get home!"

Kelly sat confused. She knew Father did not often come home on Friday nights. She paid attention to his habits. But…

"Sounds unanimous. What do you say Kelly?" Tommy pleaded. "I don't know your father, but I do know *you* and I think you deserve a night of fun. Even if you have to sneak out to have it!"

"Go Kelly," Beth urged. "I'm sure it's not a sin."

Tommy was about to question Beth but stopped when he saw Kelly sigh and nod her head yes. He leaped up, grabbed her in his arms, and spun her around. "Woo Hoo!" he shouted. She laughed loudly.

"Now that's my favorite sound!" Tommy yelled with glee and began to spin her around in a mock dance with his tall body holding onto her small frame. He spun her around and around until she collapsed in his arms like a rag doll with uncontrollable laughter. The children giggled loudly and began to dance around them to join in on the fun.

Finally pulling away from him, she asked with a big smile, "Now can we *please* finish the page in the book?"

"We sure can," he replied with a big grin and sat down with her and opened the book back up.

CHAPTER 11

The following day, Kelly was waiting at their usual rock for her reading lesson. She was beyond happy to finally be able to read even just a few sentences and it was all because of Tommy. She smiled. He was wonderful and she was so happy that God had brought him into her life. She would go to this dance with him, even if it was a huge risk, knowing he was well worth it.

"No lessons today," Tommy announced as he snuck up behind her.

"No?" she asked, plainly disappointed.

"We are going shopping," he announced with a sly grin. "Where are the kids?"

"We can't do that! Are you crazy?" she asked in a panic.

"Yes, we can Kelly. Don't worry. We will be back before…" he looked up to the sky and pointed, "before the sun is right about there."

She looked at him, embarrassed. "How did you know I can't tell time? Because I can't read?"

"No," he said teasingly. "Because you don't wear a watch!" He turned in the direction that the kids were playing and shouted, "Come on you guys! Wanna go shopping?!"

"Yes!" they both squealed.

"How do you play that?!" Billy asked happily.

Nothing surprised Tommy anymore. He just smiled and yelled "You'll see!"

"What if Father sees us?" Kelly asked.

"Don't worry. I have all the bases covered," he said. "We're going to a completely different town."

The kids were overly excited as Tommy led them off into the woods. He thanked his luck as they made their way towards his house, that the skies were overcast, and they were free from the normal lathering of mud that usually covered their skin. And knowing that their feet would probably be bare, as they always were, he had three sets of flip-flops waiting for them when they reached the house.

They tried on the flip-flops and practiced walking around the yard. Each snap that erupted from the rubber sole slapping the bottom of their bare feet caused a flurry of giggles. But it was Beth who had Tommy in stitches the most. She lifted each foot with such exaggeration, the sound created a powerful pop, and the vision made him think of a Tennessee Walking Horse with a high-stepping gait.

Still laughing at the children, Kelly reminded Tommy that they had to be back before dark. So, without further ado, he led them all to his truck in the driveway. Although it was a single cab, the four of them managed to squeeze into the front seat. Tommy knew this wasn't exactly legal, but there were plenty of back roads that he had learned to take by now to avoid being stopped by the police. But just to be extra cautious, he had the children practice ducking down on command before they set off. They spent only a few minutes on this drill before they were forced to stop due to uncontrollable laughter. Beth was apparently having a slight problem with gas and every time Billy ducked on command, the pungent odor escaped her little body, rather loudly, and invaded his breathing space. He cried out in exaggerated agony which sent Tommy, Kelly, and Beth into an involuntary laughing frenzy. And during the drive, the laughter continued. Beth was trying to hum to the music coming from the radio. Billy stared at her, with his mouth agape, as if she had completely lost her mind. Tommy saw this and so to help her out, began to belt out the country song lyrics using an exaggerated southern twang. Then Billy happily joined in and tried to mimic him with his own rendition of the song that he had never heard before. The words made no sense at all, which only heightened their laughter. Kelly could not remember having this much fun in so very long. And she knew, without a doubt, the children felt the same.

***

Bringing them to the outdoor mall about thirty miles outside of Oxville was beyond a treat for Kelly and the children. They were in awe with everything they saw. They chatted happily and touched everything that they passed. But it was the crowd of people that mostly captivated the children. They stared openly at everybody they passed. It was obvious that they had no idea that so many different types of people even existed. They occasionally glanced at Kelly looking for reassurance that this was okay. And safe. She returned their glances with as much confidence as she could, but it was all just as overwhelming for her. Without Tommy by her side, she probably would have been just as scared.

After walking for a bit, he finally stopped them in front of a pretzel vendor.

"I'm starving!" he announced and looked at them. "Who else?"

Billy and Beth both raised their hands.

"Okay!" he shouted and ordered them each an oversized pretzel. They carried them to a nearby bench and sat, holding them with such care. The moment they bit into the soft layers of buttered, salty dough, their eyes lit up. Within seconds, they had greedily devoured them, only pausing once to lick their fingers and to nod at Tommy with approval.

When they were finished, Tommy led them to their next stop. It was a colorfully lit novelty shop full of toys and trinkets.

"Pick something out," he instructed the children. Excitedly, Beth immediately went to the doll section. She chose a baby doll with curly blonde locks, bright eyes, and rosy, pink cheeks. It wore a pink, flowery dress, and dainty white stockings. She held it tight to her chest and smiled brightly. Kelly's heart melted. Beth had never owned a doll. Kelly had had them in the past, but Father had thrown them in the trash one day as punishment. It happened at the house they now lived in, shortly after Mother had left. She could not remember what she had done wrong. Only that it had devastated her.

Billy then took his turn. He walked up to a bin of toys and picked up a red whistle and eyed it curiously. Tommy laughed. "Go ahead and blow it!" Billy looked puzzled. Tommy took the whistle from his hand, put it to his own lips and blew hard into it. It sent a loud, piercing screech that rang throughout the store. The clerk, who had her back to them at the time, jumped with a startle and turned to face them. She frowned disapprovingly. They tried to conceal their giggles but were unsuccessful. Billy then took the whistle and gave it a hard blow, once again causing the clerk to frown in dismay. A big smile lit up his face.

"Oops," Tommy said to the clerk with a crooked grin. She turned her back on them and sharply stomped away.

"I'll take this!" Billy cried happily.

"For the woods only," Kelly warned, still laughing.

After purchasing the toys, Tommy led them all out of the store and showed the children a bench where they could sit and wait for them. He then took Kelly by the hand and led her into a nearby dress shop, with the children still in view. When she stepped inside, she stopped short and stared in awe at all the pretty dresses.

"Go ahead," Tommy said with a smile. "Pick one out."

She stood motionless, glancing from him to the dresses and then back to him. He looked around for a minute. He smiled again and then purposefully led her to a pretty, blue sundress that hung alone on a rack.

"What about this?" he asked, looking at the size on the dress tag and then at her slender body. "It matches your eyes. Do you like it? Would you like to try it on?"

She nodded yes and then slowly took the dress from the rack with such care one would have thought it was made of glass. A few seconds later, a tall, older woman with perfectly styled, white hair and deep red lipstick approached them. She wore a name tag on her gray blazer and Kelly immediately welled up with pride as she silently read the name, *Jean.* Jean looked down at the tattered dress that Kelly was wearing and pursed her lips in dismay. She looked back up at the two of them and forcefully changed her expression to a more welcoming tone and asked, "Can I help you?"

"Yes," Tommy cut in, "She would like to try this dress on."

Jean looked at the new dress and then directly at Kelly. It was then that she noticed the look of uncertainty and shame deep in her eyes. Sympathy washed over her and she was immediately embarrassed by her arrogance. Her shoulders dropped slightly, and her demeanor instantly softened.

"Of course," she said, more pleasantly, and then led Kelly to a nearby dressing room. Kelly took the dress into the room and closed the door behind her. When she turned to face the full-length mirror, her jaw dropped. The view before her was quite unexpected. In front of her was not the image of the young child she remembered. This person staring back at her looked more like a full-grown woman. Sadness washed over her. So many years had passed by. Years of waiting for things to get better. For things to change. She scolded herself. They *were* getting better. Tommy had come into their lives. And remembering this caused her to snap out of her self pity. She quickly undressed and slid the pretty blue dress on. Tears welled up in her eyes as she slowly spun in a circle in front of the mirror to get a good, long look at the dress on her body. She had never felt so graceful. She turned and turned, letting the folds of the dress twirl, until a tap at the door interrupted her admiration.

"Are you doing okay?" asked the nice lady named Jean.

Kelly opened the door so that Jean could see her.

"Oh, my," Jean declared. "Aren't you a pretty little thing."

Kelly smiled at her.

"Hmmm…" Jean continued. "Looks like you may need the right bra for this dress. Do you have one in mind, or would you like me to find you something?"

Kelly looked down embarrassed.

"You wait right here," Jean stated, sensing her discomfort. She closed the door for Kelly and returned a second later holding a tape measure. Kelly let Jean in the dressing room and allowed her to measure her.

"Okay," Jean said, cheerfully and left for a few more minutes. She returned with a white lace matching bra and panty set and handed it to Kelly. Once alone again, Kelly put the bra on. She had never owned one and it took her a few seconds to figure out the fasteners. She turned and turned facing the mirror again, soaking in how pretty she felt in it. But her admiration was once again interrupted when she heard Billy outside the door complaining loudly that he had to pee and wanted Tommy to hurry along. She quickly took the new things off and got back into her old garments. She carried the dress, along with the new undergarments, out of the dressing room and handed them to Jean. She looked at Tommy and smiled widely.

"I take it you approve," he stated, smiling back. "And it fits?"

"Perfectly," Jean cut in as she placed the clothes on the register to calculate the total.

Tommy walked over to the counter and pulled his wallet out. It was then he noticed the underwear. His eyebrows lifted immediately, and he glanced at Kelly and grinned widely. Her face turned red, and she quickly looked away. Jean saw this and immediately gave him a frown. Embarrassed, he quietly paid for the clothes and then took the bag and handed it to Kelly without looking at her. Kelly looked back at

Jean as they left the store and silently thanked her with her eyes. Jean smiled and gave her a gentle wave.

To top the shopping day off, Tommy pulled into a drive through ice cream stand on the way home and treated them all to a large chocolate and vanilla twist cone. The children instantly began to devour them.

"When Mother comes for us, I am gonna have one of these every day!" Billy proclaimed, in between licks. Tommy shot a curious glance at Kelly, but she pleaded with her eyes to please leave the comment alone. And knowing they were enjoying this day way too much, he abided by her silent wish.

When they pulled into Tommy's driveway, he ran through the plan with a time for the night of the dance. He would keep the dress at his house, and she could get changed and ready there.

"Oh," he said, as he reached into his pocket, "Forgot I grabbed you one more thing."

He pulled out a little box and handed it to her. She slowly opened it and inside was a dainty, silver plated watch with colorful gems that were cleverly fitted upon a stretchy wristband. She traced the pretty gems with her fingertips and looked at him and smiled sweetly. He helped her put it on and showed her where the hands on the face would be when she was to meet him at the creek. He didn't have a plan for her return home yet but was hoping somehow, she would allow him to drop her near her home, or they would have to use the headlights on the four-wheeler through the woods.

Excitement filled his head as he walked them all back to the creek to bid them a farewell. Kelly looked up at the sun and then at her new watch and smiled. He knew that the watch would mean more to her than just a pretty piece of jewelry.

CHAPTER 12

It was barely morning, and Kelly woke to the sound of shouting coming from upstairs. It was Father's voice and that of a woman. The children woke up and immediately moved closer to her. The joy from yesterday's shopping trip entered her mind momentarily, but then slowly slipped away as the shouting continued.

"You're nothing but a drunken piece of shit!" they heard the woman yell, followed by the sound of glass shattering. And then there were more sounds of a struggle. Kelly sat in fear as she heard her father roar back in anger, "You're nothing but a whore!"

"There's a lady here," Beth whispered, hopefully.

"Is it Mother?" Billy asked.

"No…I mean, I don't think so," Kelly calmly answered them, but her heart was racing. There had been women upstairs with Father before, but none this loud. Or angry. And the children were usually asleep when they were around, so they were never the wiser.

There was one woman in particular that she remembered. She could hear her coughing relentlessly upstairs, and she knew it was making Father very mad. He was shouting at her to stop and it didn't take long for the door leading outside to slam shut, indicating that they had left. How that episode did not wake the children surprised Kelly. But it was shortly after that that Beth had gotten sick, so Kelly made sure to teach her to cough into the mattress when Father was around. She did not want to anger him.

As the shouts continued upstairs, the children moved in closer to Kelly. More things were breaking, and the voices were getting louder and angrier. Suddenly the woman screamed, and the shouting stopped. They sat and listened hard, but nothing happened.

"Should we go check?" Billy asked after a minute.

Kelly looked at him. She didn't know what to do. As she was about to get up, she heard the upstairs door open, and someone take a step down. They held their breath. She dreaded Father coming down right now, so full of anger.

Just then a shiny, red, high-heeled shoe came tumbling down the basement steps and landed on the floor with a plop. Kelly looked at it and immediately thought of Dorothy's shoes from the Wizard of Oz.

"Shit!" the woman's voice yelled.

Kelly pulled the children even closer to her as they looked up to her with anticipation.

With one shoe still on, the woman slowly and clumsily made her way down the stairs while mumbling to herself the entire time. Occasionally she would lose her balance and have to sit and rest for a minute.

"All men should be shot," she said under her breath as she reached the bottom step and sat down to retrieve her shoe. "Talking to me like that. I ain't gonna put up with that shit," she continued, as she fumbled with the shoe. "I'll put this shoe so far up your ass, you'll be tasting your shit for a month."

Billy let out an involuntary giggle and Kelly quickly put her hand over his mouth.

The woman stopped, looked in their direction, and squinted.

"Somebody down here?" she asked, suspiciously.

They all sat quietly. She stood up and with one high heeled shoe on her foot and the other dangling from her hand, she awkwardly made her way to them. Her silhouette rose and fell with each step, making Kelly think of a pirate and it unnerved her even more.

When she was fully in sight, she stopped suddenly, and her jaw dropped.

"Well, what-a-we got here?"

None of them spoke. The woman's jet-black hair was wildly tousled, and her eyes were painted in bright blue colors with dark lines around them. Her red blouse showed a lot of her skin, and her black, shiny pants looked as though they might split at any minute. Kelly could smell her strong perfume. It engulfed them like a wall, but it definitely improved the basement's usual odor. This, undoubtedly, was not Mother.

"Hey," she said, with a slur, and as she took a step forward, lost her balance and fell forward. She landed on the mattress beside them and laughed heartily as she struggled to sit up. Billy and Beth giggled with her. Kelly squeezed their hands in warning.

"Who are you kids? Is that your old man upstairs?"

They did not answer her.

"Well, if he is, I'm sorry, but he's a real nut case!"

Kelly darted her eyes towards the stairs. If Father heard this, he would surely lose his mind. The woman noticed this and patted her on the hand. "Now don't you worry about him, Dolly, I done knocked him out cold! Never underestimate a cast iron skillet in a lady's hand that don't cook!" She laughed loudly at her own statement and Kelly couldn't help but smile. The woman glanced around the basement and tsked. "Shit. And I thought it was bad upstairs. What're you kids doing down here?"

Still, they would not respond.

"Well, I'm Ruby," she continued. "Ruby Red is what they call me."

"Like Dorothy's slippers," Kelly said, quietly, and then instantly regretted sharing her thoughts.

"*Dorothy?*" Ruby asked, "'That another woman he got comin' around here? Somebody out there as crazy as me?"

"From the Wizard of Oz," Kelly hurriedly explained.

Ruby let out a loud, boisterous laugh. "Sweety, this ain't no land of Oz, I can promise you that! More like the House of Horrors!"

She didn't understand what she meant but couldn't help but smile at her anyway. She had an infectious laugh that contagiously spread and touched each of them.

Ruby caught Beth staring at the gold chain, adorned with a gold, half-moon pendant, dangling from her neck.

"You like this?" Ruby asked her and held the pendant up. Beth shyly shook her head yes.

"Well," Ruby said, "It's yours." She lifted the necklace off her own neck and leaned over to drape it around Beth's neck. It hung down and came close to touching her belly button. Beth reached down and lifted the pendant up to her face to get a better look at it and smiled.

"It's supposed to give you inner power. Not exactly working for me!" Ruby said and burst out laughing again. "Do yourself a favor, love, and don't go depending on no man when you grow up. Get yourself a career. And I don't mean one like the one I got! Oh, hell no!"

Beth shook her head in agreement, but it was clear that she had no idea what Ruby meant. Kelly decided to let Beth wear the necklace for a little while until it was time to stow it away in the hiding place.

"Someday," Ruby said, and stared off into the basement as if in deep thought," Gonna get me a real job." She reached around behind her to pull out a flattened pack of cigarettes from her back pocket. "And a real house." She pulled a cigarette out of the pack and managed to mold it back into shape before lighting it. She took a deep drag and then offered it to Kelly. Kelly immediately nodded her head no, but before Ruby could put the cigarette back to her mouth, Billy reached out and took it from her. He put it to his mouth and mimicked what he had seen her do. Immediately, he burst into a coughing fit. Ruby laughed loudly and took the cigarette back from him.

"You don't want to get started on these, Darlin.' They'll kill you. Fixin' to quit myself someday," she said with a smile and inhaled again.

"Gonna get me a dog," she continued, as she exhaled. "And a pool." She looked back at the children. "What do you think? If I get me a pool, ya wanna come over and swim?"

"Yes," Billy and Beth replied in unison. Kelly smiled. She knew they had no idea what Ruby was talking about. They only wanted to do something. *Anything.*

Ruby finished her smoke, snuffed it out on the floor and as she tried to hoist herself up off the mattress, the button on her blouse broke free and her rather large, left bare breast spilled out. Billy caught his breath and gawked openly at it with wide eyes. She laughed loudly again and as she tried to cover it, she said to him. "Now sweety, you never mind. That's gonna control you soon enough someday." As she continued to fumble with her blouse again, a loud commotion came from upstairs.

"Shit," she said as she clumsily lifted herself up off the mattress and put her other shoe on. "Sleeping beauty must have come to. Gonna get his hairy ass to take me home now."

Beth gasped and Ruby immediately corrected herself and said, "Butt."

Kelly and Billy both giggled.

She straightened her blouse and smiled warmly at the three of them. "Make sure you get yourselves upstairs. It's cold down here." Kelly nodded to imply that they would, but of course, that was not an option.

She managed to make her way back up the stairs and as soon as she reached the top, they could hear Father bellow from the top of his lungs.

"What the hell were you doing down there?!"

They waited for a clever response, but none came. Maybe they were done being mad at each other, Kelly decided. And after what seemed like a very long time, they finally heard the door to the outside close.

"I like Ruby," Billy said to Kelly, and smiled.

"And I think Ruby can beat Father's ass," Beth added, innocently.

"Beth!" Kelly said with surprise and then giggled again.

"You mean his hairy ass," Billy wittingly added.

She looked at both the children and smiled. She liked Ruby too and hoped that maybe one day she would visit them again. And if anything, she thought with amusement, she could teach the children a few more new words.

CHAPTER 13

"Damn, Owens, you're on fire!" Riley shouted, as Tommy scored his fifth goal to win the game. They gave each other a high five and ran off the field to join the handshake line as the crowd excitedly applauded them.

"Owens," Riley said breathlessly as they finished the handshakes and headed back to the bench, "There's a party tonight. You gotta go!"

Tommy looked at him and indecisively pursed his lips. Without answering him he turned to scan the crowd for his parents with no luck. They both had gotten to know a few of the parents and kids while attending his games, so he just assumed they were off chatting somewhere.

"What do ya say?" Riley continued excitedly, "Cheap liquor, cheap woman. Let's go destroy this town!" He outstretched his arms, balled his fists, and began to wildly jerk his hips like a dog in heat. Tommy looked behind him and widened his eyes. Riley spun around quickly, and his jaw dropped when he saw Nancy standing there, just two feet away, with her arms crossed and a look on her face that clearly stated that she was not pleased with his idea.

"Mrs. Owens!" he quickly said. "How lovely it is to see you. Of course, you know I was just being silly. Your son and I would never partake in that kind of disgusting behavior. I was really thinking more of a good wholesome movie or a trip to the library."

"Now, that sounds nice," she replied, naively.

Pete gave Tommy a smirk and then slapped him on the back.

"Good game, son. You too, Riley."

"Why, thank you, Mr. Owens," Riley answered, continuing with his innocent act.

Just then one of the cheerleaders bounced by and stopped when she saw Riley. She gave him a mischievous grin, turned her back to him and flipped her black and gold cheerleading skirt up and shook her rear at him. Another cheerleader trotted by, grabbed her by the arm, and they both ran off giggling.

Riley just stood there with a deep look of concern on his face and pursed his lips.

"These kids," he finally said and shook his head with disgust.

"Wasn't that Tina?" Nancy asked, confused.

"It was," Riley answered as he bobbed his head, still feigning concern.

"And isn't she your girlfriend?"

"She is."

Tommy burst out laughing, unable to play along with Riley's comical charade any longer.

Riley looked at him, pretending to be confused and then tried again. "So, what do you think, Thomas? You in?"

Tommy figured it wouldn't hurt to hang out with Riley for the rest of the evening. If anything, he would certainly keep him amused.

"Sure," he replied.

"That sounds wonderful!" Nancy said. "Just behave and be *safe*." She reached up to kiss him on the cheek.

Slightly embarrassed, he looked at Riley. But that quickly passed when Riley slumped down to Nancy's height, turned his cheek and tapped it with his fingertip. She smiled and reached up to give him a kiss on the cheek as well.

***

"Where we going?" Tommy asked with confusion, as he continued down the road. He had decided to drive for two reasons. One, he didn't plan on drinking and two, more obviously, Riley didn't own a vehicle.

"Just up the road," Riley promised as he scrolled through the stations on the radio. Finally settling on a classic rock song, he cranked up the volume and began to beat his hands on the dash in an attempt to mimic the pounding drum sound.

"What house am I looking for?!" Tommy tried to yell over the music.

"What?!" Riley yelled back.

Tommy reached over and turned the music down slightly and repeated, "What house am I looking for?"

Riley looked out Tommy's window and abruptly shouted, "Here! Right there!"

Tommy quickly put on the breaks and looked around. He looked at the houses but couldn't find any with a group of cars in the driveway indicating a sign of a party. He turned back to Riley. "Which house?"

"Not a house. Right there," he said, and pointed.

Tommy looked at where he was pointing. All he could see was a library.

"You're serious?" he asked and laughed.

"Trust me, dude, just pull in the driveway and follow it around the back."

Tommy did as he was told and once he made his way around the back, he could see a few cars with kids climbing out and heading into the woods behind it. Riley looked at him and smirked. "You don't think I would lie to your mother, do you?"

Tommy laughed, parked the truck, and they both climbed out. Riley grabbed his mini cooler from the back of the truck, and they headed down a path leading into the woods. After a short distance, they came upon a clearing in a field. Tommy could see a rather large group of kids standing around a large bonfire, chatting, and sipping drinks. There were benches made from logs scattered about and a large boombox sat off to the side blaring an old-time country rock song.

Riley set his cooler down, reached in to pull out a can of beer, and then lifted it high in the air.

"Welcome to the library!" he said and laughed as they headed toward the fire.

Tommy immediately recognized a few of the guys from the team so he wandered over to join them. After about twenty minutes of conversation that consisted mostly of soccer and opposing team players, he glanced around for Riley. Although they hadn't been there that long, he was feeling like he might be ready to leave. He spotted him sitting on a log with Tina on his lap, and another girl sitting close by. Riley looked at him and flagged him over. As he drew closer, he saw the other girl lean in and whisper to Tina, causing her to smile mischievously.

"Tom," Riley said, and patted a spot on the log next to him. "Come join us."

Tommy sat down and gave a quick wave to the girls.

"Do you know Melanie?" Tina asked and gestured to the girl sitting beside her. He looked at her and she smiled. He had seen her around school but was never formally introduced.

"Hi," he said, politely. "Tom."

Tina burst out laughing. "Who doesn't know that Mr. Super Star?!"

Riley faked a frown and deepened his voice. "Hey, calm down there little Missie. You're taken."

Tina laughed again, leaned down to kiss him, and then lifted her head up to his ear to whisper something in it. He looked at Tommy and then Melanie and then back to Tina and shook his head no. Tina giggled again and then said under her breath, with a pout, "You're no fun."

Riley pursed his lips, growled, and then stood up with Tina still in his arms. She giggled loudly as he carried her away and headed toward the woods.

Tommy looked around awkwardly. Now he *really* wanted to leave. He glanced at Melanie from the corner of his eye to see if she too might be feeling awkward and ready to part ways, but her long, mousy brown hair shielded her eyes, making it hard to read her expression. She had a bottle of whiskey in her hand that she occasionally brought to her lips to sip on. He could tell she was tipsy by the way she unsteadily swayed as she sat there. He sat for a few minutes longer and still she made no effort to get up from the log. Not wanting to be rude, he turned to her and asked, "So, you're a junior? Thought I might have seen you in the fifth period lunchroom."

"Yeah," she said and grinned.

He looked around again. Just a few more minutes of small talk and he could bow out gracefully.

"Are you going to the dance next week? I hear it's supposed to be a lot of fun," he continued, dully.

"Yes," she said quickly.

"Good, maybe I'll…"

"Yes, I'll go with you!" she gushed excitedly.

Shit. This certainly took a wrong turn, he thought. He ran his fingers through his hair wondering how he was gonna let her down. She obviously misunderstood his intent and now he feared she might feel like a fool. Or, he thought, he could just say nothing in the hope that she might not even remember this conversation tomorrow, but that was too big of a gamble.

A few kids walked past them and looked at Melanie and then at Tommy with surprise. He wasn't sure what the looks were about, but he thought it was best to wait until they were out of earshot before he broke the news. And just as he was about to let her know about Kelly, Dan slowly strutted by and looked at them.

"Owens!" he shouted and laughed loudly. "You two make a good couple!" He paused for a second and then finished, "A couple of whack jobs!"

Tommy didn't respond. Nothing Dan said bothered him anymore. But when he glanced back at Melanie, he could tell that the comment definitely upset her, and *that* bothered him. He stood up and glared at Dan.

Dan burst out laughing. "Whoa! You're gonna fight over *her*? Damn, Owens, you are desperate."

Tommy continued to stare him down until he slowly turned away.

"Not gonna waste my time on this one," Dan said as he walked away, laughing. "You already got your hands full." He stopped and turned back to look at Melanie and gave her a wink. "Let me know if you need a ride home."

Tommy looked back at Melanie. She seemed pleased that he had stood up to Dan for her. She smiled and looked at him with a gleam in her eyes. *Shit* he thought again. He had better set the situation straight and do it quickly. He waited a few minutes before nervously saying to her, "Um, about the dance, the thing is…I already have a date."

Her demeanor instantly changed, and she looked at him doubtfully. "I never saw you with anybody," she said with annoyance.

"Well, she doesn't come to our school," he quickly responded, wondering why she suddenly scared him.

"Of course, she doesn't," she said, sarcastically.

An infuriating expression crossed over her face, and she glared at him. Deciding not to fuel her anger any further, he turned to walk away.

"Where is she tonight?" She pressed loudly. "Probably out whoring' around with somebody else," she spat.

His blood began to boil, and he turned to glare back at her.

She abruptly stood up, and before he could set her straight, she stormed off and headed toward the woods that led back to the library. She stopped only once and that was to turn around and shout back to him, "Liar! You're a fucking liar!"

He stood there astonished. *What in the hell just happened?!*

A few of his teammates wandered by and snickered.

"See ya met Melanie!" one yelled out to him and laughed.

He stood there shaking his head in disbelief. This was exactly why he was more than happy to just stay home. He thought about Kelly. *Life was so much easier with Kelly.*

"What did you say to her?" Tina laughed with bewilderment when she and Riley came back to join him.

He lifted his arms up in wonderment. "What the hell was that all about?" he asked and looked at Riley.

"Sorry, man. It was her," he replied and nodded towards Tina. "She can be a little mean sometimes."

"Just trying to have a little fun," Tina said as she smacked Riley in the arm. "Sorry, Tommy," she said, and looked at him. "That wasn't very nice of me. She's a little on the unstable side. Whatever you said, really pissed her off, though. She said, *I mean screamed*, that she was walking home. And she lives two miles from here!"

"You're not friends?" Tommy asked, confused.

"*Friends?!*" Tina scoffed. "She doesn't have any friends. She'll snap on you in a heartbeat! But of course, you know that now."

Tommy sighed and shook his head. "How'd she get here?"

"She always gets a ride. The guys will bring her. She supplies the bottles, and some other choice favors, and they supply the ride. She lives with her grandfather, who always has his liquor cabinet stocked. And he's oblivious. I don't even know if he even knows she lives with him," she finished and chuckled.

"She's had a tough life," Riley said with a little compassion. "Her parents died in a wreck that she survived and she aint been the same since. I kinda feel sorry for her."

Tommy nodded his head to him. "Yeah. Well, I think I've had enough for tonight. I'm gonna head out. You coming?"

"Are you really pissed?"

"No, we're good. Just wanna head home."

"Okay. I'm gonna catch a ride with Tina. Talk to you later, buddy," Riley finished and reached out to give him a side hug.

***

Tommy took a slow ride home. Even though Melanie had freaked out on him, he still felt sorry for her, and it bothered him. He knew firsthand how trauma could change a person. Of course, Nancy's change was not as eccentric, but it still changed her.

Knowing that a two-mile walk would still leave her walking down the dark road at this time, he took his time and kept an alert eye on the shoulder. He had no idea where she lived, so after about three miles, he turned around and went in the opposite direction.

After driving for about two more miles, he glanced out the side window to look at the full moon for a second. But it was a second too long. Something large slammed into and rolled up on the hood of his truck before falling back off causing him to slam on the brakes in a panic. He sat for a moment in the middle of the road as horrible thoughts raced through his mind. *Was it a person?*

He took a deep breath and then reached in his glove box for a flashlight. Then he slowly got out of the truck and proceeded to shine the light around the general area. And then he spotted it. A large, dark, indistinct shape lying motionless on the side of the road. He took another deep breath and cautiously approached it and upon closer inspection, relief swept over him. It was only a deer.

He wasn't sure how to handle the situation. This never happened in the streets of Chicago, but he decided the best thing was to lift the deer off the road and perhaps take it home to properly dispose of it. He got back in his truck to back it up as close as he could and then proceeded to hoist the deer into the bed of his truck, which he quickly learned was no easy feat.

When he got home, he pulled the deer out of the bed of the truck and dragged it around to the side of the barn and left it in the weeds. It was late and he promised himself that he would somehow take care of it in the morning. But right now, he was exhausted. Physically and emotionally. The dead deer bothered him and even though he knew deer were commonly hunted in this area, he couldn't help but feel sadness. And then there was Melonie. He had to guess, or hope, that she had gotten a ride home somehow and was now safe.

CHAPTER 14

It was Saturday morning, and Tommy woke to a chorus of birds chirping outside his window. He climbed out of bed and leisurely walked over to the window to lift it fully open. A cool gentle breeze burst in, filling the room with a crisp, clean scent that immediately overpowered the aroma of his gym bag lying in the corner and the funky smell of teenage sweat. The sun was just rising with the promise of a nice day, so he wasted no time heading downstairs to begin his day.

Nancy and Pete were already up sipping coffee and reading the newspaper in the sunroom. He grabbed a glass of orange juice and headed in to join them.

"Morning, son," Pete said, pleasantly.

Nancy glanced up from her paper and gave him a melancholy smile. She was in one of her quiet moods and it looked as though she might have been crying.

"Everything okay?" Tommy gently asked her.

She just looked at him and frowned.

"Your mother's friend passed away last night," Pete answered, for her. "Anna."

Tommy looked at him surprised. "But she's a doctor," he said with confusion.

"Doctors are people too," Pete stated plainly. "She had a hemorrhagic stroke."

Tommy put his juice down and walked over to wrap his arms around Nancy's shoulders.

"I'm so sorry," he murmured softly to her.

"I know," she responded quietly and rose to leave the room. "I just need some time alone."

Tommy tilted his head and looked at Pete bewildered.

"She'll be okay," Pete assured him.

Tommy nodded and left to head back upstairs for a shower. He felt bad for his mother. She and Anna had been friends since high school, and he could only imagine how hard it must be to lose a close friend like that. Although he hadn't spent a whole lot of time with Anna, he could remember her being very kind. And she proved to still be with the favor she had done to help Beth.

After a shower and a bowl of cereal, Tommy headed outside. He decided to head down to the creek just in case Kelly and the kids were there. It was always a hit or miss with them but that didn't stop him from trying anyway.

To his delight, they were there, and Kelly's face brightened when he approached.

"Good morning," he said with a smile in his voice. "I'm so happy you're here."

"Me too. Father said he will be gone for a couple of days so we can play for as long as we want today! *And* I don't have to make supper for him."

"You cook?" he asked her teasingly.

"Of course!"

"I try, but my mother usually pushes me away. I either use too much salt or too much sugar or too much of pretty much anything," he said and chuckled.

She laughed with him. "Your mother is a very good cook."

He smiled and looked at her and then an idea popped into his mind. Maybe a visit from Kelly and the kids could help cheer Nancy up. It sounded like they had the entire day free.

"Why don't you guys come over for lunch today?" he asked with eagerness. "Mom's feeling kinda sad and I think seeing you guys might cheer her up!"

Kelly looked at him thoughtfully. He took that as a yes and turned to yell excitedly to Billy and Beth, "Come on guys! We're gonna hang out at my pad!"

"Yay!" they shouted in unison and came running to him.

"What's your pad?" Billy asked, breathlessly.

"It's a bed, silly," Beth answered him.

Tommy laughed. "My house."

"Yes!" he yelled.

***

When they got to Tommy's house, Nancy was swaying on the porch swing with a blanket draped over her lap. She saw them come around the front of the house and her face instantly beamed with happiness.

"I brought some lunch guests, if that's okay," Tommy said to her with a grin.

She rose and smiled widely at them.

"Of course. It is a little early for lunch right now, but never too early for cookies. Anybody interested in helping me bake some?"

Beth immediately raised her hand.

"Well, come on then!" Nancy said and gestured to them to follow her into the house.

As Kelly, Beth, and Billy began to follow her, Billy stopped and turned to look at Tommy. "Aren't you coming?"

"Nah," he said. "I think I'm gonna give that tire swing over there a try."

Billy looked at the tire swing and his face lit up.

"Can I help?" he asked Tommy.

"Help? You're gonna push me!"

"Yes!" he shouted and ran to the swing with Tommy close behind him.

After close to an hour of non-stop swinging, Tommy suggested they kick the soccer ball around for a bit. He led Billy into the barn to get the ball, but Billy became immediately fascinated by the barn's contents instead. He wandered around touching things and asking endless questions. When he spotted the four-wheeler, he looked at Tommy with curiosity.

"Go ahead," Tommy told him. "Climb up on it."

Billy climbed up on the seat and smiled widely at him. Tommy then squeezed in front of him and started the engine.

"Now, hang on!" He warned him and backed the machine out of the barn. He took him for a ride through the yard and then through the woods for a bit and then back to the yard. Billy squealed the entire time, and Tommy could tell that he was enjoying himself immensely.

When they finally pulled the machine back into the barn and got off, Billy spotted a BB gun leaning in the corner. He ran to it and picked it up.

"Whoa, hold on, partner," Tommy said and quickly grabbed the gun from his hands. "Do you know what this is?"

Billy nodded his head yes.

"Have you ever shot one?"

He nodded his head no.

"Okay," Tommy continued, "They can be very dangerous. If you're careful, we could give it a try."

"Okay," Billy answered, excitedly.

Just then Pete walked in the barn and asked sternly, "What's going on in here?"

"Tommy said we can give it a try," Billy quickly answered nervously.

"No," Pete answered flatly and watched Billy's face drop. "Not without some cans to shoot at!" he finished jokingly and reached out to tousle his hair.

Tommy laughed and led Billy to the recycle bin so that they could grab a handful of empty soda cans to take back to the front yard. They placed the empty cans in a straight line around twenty-five yards away from their intended shooting point and then Pete gave Billy a lesson on safety and shooting.

Billy was having a hard time hitting the cans and Pete and Tommy were only able to average one out of every five shots. They laughed at each other's lack of talent for a while and just when Pete decided that maybe they should move a little closer to their target, Nancy and the girls came out of the house carrying a plate of cookies.

"Break time!" Tommy shouted when he saw the cookies and he and Billy ran up on the porch to grab one from the plate, leaving Pete to carry the gun. Nancy looked at the gun and then at Pete and raised her eyebrows with concern.

"I'm not sure if I'm thrilled with this," she murmured to him.

"We're being careful," he assured her.

"Whatcha doing?" Beth asked, as she looked down at the gun and then the cans.

"We're shootin'!" Billy said excitedly.

"Can I try?" she asked.

"I think it's only for boys," he replied.

Beth frowned and looked at Nancy and Kelly. Kelly shrugged her shoulders, not sure how to respond. A pitiful look crossed Nancy's face and then she pursed her lips and thought for a second.

"Nonsense," she finally said, sternly. "No such thing as only for boys. I think Beth can try if she'd like."

Pete gave Nancy a look of surprise and then turned to Beth. "Well, come on then. Let's see you give it a try."

Beth followed him out into the yard. He gave her the same safety tips that he had given Billy and showed her how to hold the gun and aim. She kneeled and shot but her first shot came nowhere near the cans. She looked at Pete with disappointment.

"Close one eye," he suggested.

She pumped the gun and tried again. A ping erupted from one of the cans as it flipped into the air and dropped.

"Wow!" Pete and Tommy yelled, in unison.

She pumped again and shot and once again a can went spinning in the air. She shot four more times, and each shot hit its target. She stood up smiling and handed the gun back to Pete. He slowly took it and looked at Tommy with amazement, who was clearly just as impressed.

"We've got ourselves a sharpshooter!" Pete exclaimed.

She looked around at everybody and beamed with pride. They all seemed to share in her joy. Except for Billy. He looked a little perturbed that his sister had shown him up. She went to him, still smiling and wrapped an arm around him.

"I bet you're pretty good, too," she said to him. Quickly changing his demeanor, he grinned sheepishly and returned her hug.

As Tommy went to gather the cans, the sound of tires pulling in at the end of the driveway suddenly caught their attention. Panic instantly gripped Kelly and she quickly rushed to grab Billy and Beth by the hand and lead them up on the porch and into the house. Tommy hurried to catch up with them, leaving Nancy and Pete standing there confused.

"What's going on?" Tommy asked her with concern once they were in the house.

"We can't be seen here," she gushed as the children moved in closer to her. "Father can't find out."

"Okay, okay," he said, trying to calm her. "We can just wait here. I'm sure it's nobody important."

They quietly stood in the kitchen for a few minutes until they heard Pete yell from outside, "Tommy! Come out here!"

He looked at Kelly. "Just wait here. It'll be okay."

When he got outside, he found Sheriff Brady standing by his cruiser with Pete and Nancy. He cautiously walked over to them.

"Sheriff here says he has a few questions for you," Pete said with concern.

"Hope I'm not bothering you," Brady stated as he twirled a toothpick around in his mouth.

"No, sir, just inside doing homework." he answered and then darted his eyes at Pete and Nancy, in an attempt to warn them to leave Kelly and the children out of the conversation.

"Ah, good," Brady said and then glanced over to the pile of cans. He sighed and then turned back to Tommy. "You know Melanie Burrows?"

Tommy looked at him confused. The only Melanie he knew was the Melanie he had met last night. And he didn't know her last name. "Um, I'm not sure. Should I?"

"Apparently you spent some time with her last night?" Brady continued.

The question made him nervous. *What did that matter?* "Yea," he finally answered, "I chatted with her for a bit, I guess."

Brady spit the toothpick on the ground. "She missed her counseling appointment this morning. According to her grandfather, she never made it home last night. Of course, he wouldn't have known if I hadn't stopped in. Anyway, I know it hasn't been twenty-four hours yet, but I didn't think it could hurt to ask a few questions this morning."

Tommy shrugged his shoulders, confused.

"I hear you were the last one to see her?" Brady continued.

"I don't really know her. She left the…" he paused and looked at his mother, "library by herself."

"Hmm..." Brady snickered, apparently familiar with the library, and looked around the yard before pointing to Tommy's truck. "That's your truck over there?"

Tommy nodded and Brady began to slowly walk over to it with Tommy, Pete, and Nancy following behind him. When they reached it, Brady pointed to the dent in the hood. He looked curiously at Tommy.

"I hit a deer last night," Tommy quickly said.

Nancy gasped. "Sorry," he said and looked back at his parents. "It was late when I got home, and I forgot to mention it this morning."

Brady walked around to the back of the truck. Tommy's heart dropped when he spotted the blood that Brady was inspecting. It certainly didn't look good.

"From the deer," he rushed. "It's around back."

He led Brady around to the back of the barn and a putrid smell immediately hit them. The doe lay there with its face bloodied and its belly fully bloated. He turned to see Nancy gag and then quickly leave the scene.

"You might want to get this taken care of," Brady said, "Gonna bring the coyotes around."

"We will," Pete said and sternly looked at Tommy.

Satisfied, Brady turned to head back to his cruiser. "If you have any ideas about the girl, let me know," he said and looked at Tommy. "She's been known to disappear sometimes for days, but we always have to check."

"I will," Tommy said.

After Brady left, Pete looked at Tommy. "Hopefully, whoever the girl is, she's okay. You don't know anything?"

"No Dad. All I know is that she has some real issues."

"Okay," Pete said. "You need to talk to us about stuff. We can't help if we don't know what's going on."

Tommy nodded and Pete continued, "Now let's get that deer cleaned up."

"Okay," he answered. "I'm just gonna check on Kelly and the kids first."

He went into the house and found Kelly standing with Nancy. She had a worried look on her face.

"It's okay," he assured her.

"I can't find the kids," Kelly said in a panic.

"What do you mean?"

"I just got in here and found her hiding in the bathroom," Nancy cut in.

"I told the kids to hide when I heard the door opening," Kelly rushed, "And I ran to the bathroom, but they didn't follow me."

"We'll find them," he assured her. "The house isn't that big."

They split up and proceeded to search the house. They looked behind the furniture and inside closets and still could not find them. Tommy stood confused. And it was then that he could hear the faint sound of voices coming from the second floor. He ran up the stairs to find that the voices were coming from his bedroom. When he entered the room, he discovered his television was on, but the children were nowhere in sight. He first checked in his closet, with no luck, and then wandered around the room for a second before finally bending down to look under his bed. And there they were, hiding under the bed with just enough of their faces peeping out from under the ruffle to be able to see the television. He burst out laughing.

"You can come out now!" he said to them.

Nancy and Kelly entered the room as the children crawled out.

"You put the TV on before hiding?" Nancy laughed. "That's not very sneaky."

"How did you know how to do that?" Kelly asked.

Nancy and Tommy looked at her confused but did not comment.

"We saw Tommy do it downstairs last time," Billy answered.

Kelly nodded her head in understanding, but Tommy was confused. He thought *everybody* owned a television but apparently Kelly's family did not. And although he knew the children didn't attend a school, they were certainly far from dumb.

They finally headed back downstairs, and Tommy left the three of them with Nancy while he went outside to help Pete take care of the deer.

"So, what should we have for lunch?" Nancy asked them, with a smile back on her face.

Kelly and Beth shrugged, but Billy raised his hand.

"Yes, Billy?" Nancy chuckled. "You have an idea?"

"Yea," he replied. "Can we watch some more TV?"

CHAPTER 15

The days leading up to the big dance were filled with reading lessons, fun, and laughter by the creek. When the day had finally arrived, Kelly found herself anticipating this special time with Tommy so much that she continuously found herself sneaking into the secret hiding spot to check the hands on her new watch.

And it had finally come. Father's dinner was cleverly placed in the crockpot she had found in the back of one of his cupboards. Why she had not found this sooner after all these years, was beyond her. But the important thing was that she found it before this special night. She hugged the children tightly and reminded them to be extra quiet if Father came home. They promised they would and off she went, through the window, and down to the creek.

Tommy was waiting with a glorious grin. He took her by the hand, and they practically skipped to his four-wheeler to race off toward his home.

Nancy was ready for Kelly when they arrived and led her straight upstairs to the master bathroom. Kelly turned the shower on, stepped in, and tilted her head back to allow her body to swallow in the steady and intense spray of warm water. Years of neglect and filth slowly slid from her skin. She reached for the soap and began to lather and vigorously scrub herself, only stopping occasionally to breathe in deep the lavish scent. When she was fully satisfied that she was clean, she let the water pour down and over her body to rinse and caress every inch of herself. She could have stayed there forever relishing in its comfort but fearing that she had taken too much time already she reluctantly turned the water off and stepped out of the shower. She found the plush bath towel and robe that Nancy had left for her draped over the sink. She dried herself quickly and put on the robe before peeking her head out of the bathroom door to find Nancy waiting patiently.

Nancy then led her into her master bedroom and motioned for her to sit in the seat at the dressing table and began to blow dry her long blond hair. When she was done, she styled some soft curls into them with a curling wand. It was obvious that she was enjoying this immensely by the pretty tune she hummed during the entire process.

Kelly had not felt this cared for in so very long. A tear formed in her eye as a memory of Mother flashed before her doing this very thing.

"Let's make your hair nice and pretty," Mother had said with a smile as she finished putting one braid on the side of Kelly's long hair.

"Where are you?! I've been calling for you!" Father had yelled as he came into the bathroom.

"I have to finish her hair before the bus comes."

"I'll finish it!" he roared as he reached onto the top shelf to grab a pair of scissors and with one swift lop, the braid fell to the floor. Kelly cried out as he took Mother's arm and yanked her from the bathroom.

"Kelly?" Nancy called, taking her from her thoughts.

Kelly looked up at her and feigned a smile.

"We're almost done," Nancy said with concern as she studied her face. "Are you okay?"

When Kelly nodded that she was, Nancy reached down to retrieve her makeup bag from the middle shelf on her table and stopped again to stare at Kelly's face.

"Well, this certainly isn't necessary," she said, with assurance. "You are truly blessed with natural beauty." Nonetheless, she dabbed some blush on Kelly's cheeks, put a quick coat of mascara on her already long, dark lashes, and glossed her lips. She put the bag back on the table and nodded in approval, signaling that the pampering was finally finished. She then left the room so that Kelly could put on the underwear set, the pretty blue dress, and a pair of soft brown, leather sandals that Nancy had been able to scurry up for her.

When Kelly finished dressing, she walked over to look into Nancy's full-length mirror. Her heart skipped a beat when she saw the image that stood before her. There she was, just as she remembered her, *Mother.* Kelly closed her eyes and took a deep breath, feeling that perhaps her eyes were playing tricks on her. But when she opened them back up, the same image remained.

"Absolutely beautiful," Nancy said as she stepped back into the room, interrupting her thoughts. She walked over and gave her a soft hug. Another tear began to slip from Kelly's eye.

"Now, now," Nancy said with a smile. "You don't want to redden those beautiful blue eyes."

Tommy was downstairs pacing the floor when he heard the two finally come down the stairs. He looked up and his heart stopped.

Descending the steps was the most beautiful girl he had ever seen. She looked angelic as she smiled sweetly down at him.

"Well?" Nancy asked. "How does your date look?"

He could barely speak and when he finally did, it came out in a low murmur. "Okay."

Nancy laughed. "Okay? I thought you might approve," she said, knowingly and continued, "Your father and I have a dinner party to attend this evening. They are honoring him and his staff for the tremendous work they have done on the new plant. So, we will probably be home late. You two have fun, but most importantly, be safe." She reached up to kiss him on the cheek and then walked over to do the same for Kelly. An incredible smile spread across Kelly's face.

"Thank you," she quietly said as Tommy took her by the hand and led her out the door with his face beaming.

***

The gymnasium at the school was pounding with the sound of loud rock music, boisterous laughs, and happy chatter. Kelly looked around in fascination. All the balloons and decorations were glorious, but seeing all the girls that looked like they were near her age was captivating. So many of them. All looking so very pretty and so happy. How she wished she could be friends with even just one of them.

Tommy caught her staring at them and leaned down to whisper in her ear, "You are the prettiest one here. I promise you that." He smiled at her and gently circled her waist with his arm and pulled her closer to him. He welled up with pride noticing all the envious stares.

But there was one stare, in particular, that overpowered them all. And that was the stare of Catrina. And that stare got harder and harder the more Dan looked over to glance at Kelly with approval.

"Come on," Tommy said to Kelly as he led her to the dance floor. The band was playing a rendition of Bryan Adams' "Heaven". He gently lifted her arms so that she could cradle his neck and then he put his hands softly around her waist. He gently swayed to the music, and it wasn't long before she caught on and followed his movement. They danced slowly and looked into each other's eyes, lost in what Kelly found to be the most wonderful feeling that she had ever experienced.

97

She knew then and there that this moment would live in her mind and heart forever. She smiled up at him and he looked deeply into her eyes and then softly whispered, "I love you, Kelly."

Her eyes grew wide as she stared back at him. He was just as surprised as her with what had just come out of his mouth. But he said it. And he meant it. His heart had spoken out loud and there was no taking it back. He only hoped it would not upset her.

Her heart was pounding, and she felt as though she might burst. *He loved her*. This bond they shared felt so natural and easy. What else could this be, but love?

"And I love you Tommy," she finally whispered back.

The words poured into his ears and pulled his mouth into a wide grin.

He lifted her up in his arms and spun her around. They both laughed until he gently set her back down. She laid her head on his chest, and they continued to sway to the music, holding each other tight.

When the song ended, he led her to a table to get some punch and to explore the large spread of hors d'oeuvres. Kelly wasted no time filling a plate with grapes, cheese, and crackers. Tommy began to tease her at the way she was greedily devouring the snacks. She laughed with him and to show him she was not offended, grabbed a handful of the crackers, and teasingly pressed them to his mouth, causing them to crumble, stick to his lips, and then slide down the front of his shirt. He drew back, wiping the crackers from his mouth and laughed with her. Then they playfully took turns throwing grapes into each other's mouths, mostly unsuccessful, until Tommy could no longer wait to reach out and wrap his arms around her once again. Nothing, he decided, could break this bubble that engulfed them.

They were eventually joined by Riley and his date, along with a few of his other friends. He introduced Kelly to them, and she immediately became a magnet of intrigue. She smiled widely the whole time, responding vaguely, but politely, to their curious questions. As she stood savoring all the attention she was unexpectedly receiving, Tommy couldn't help but grin from ear to ear. He could not have been prouder as she stood by his side and everything about this night was perfect.

That was until he was suddenly jerked around from behind. Catrina had him by the arm and with a big, confident grin, leaned into him and said, "Come on. My turn for that kind of dance." She had on a short, black, strapless dress that she, no doubt, had to pry herself into and her perfume was so loud that he had to turn his face to the side to keep from choking. He backed away, pulled his arm from her, and returned his attention to Kelly.

But Catrina would not be ignored. She wedged herself between Tommy and Kelly and pressed her body against him. He angrily took a step back only to be stopped abruptly by Dan's solid stance. He quickly turned and glared at him. Dan returned the glare and then snorted. "Whatcha got going here, city boy? You movin' in on my girl?" He smelled of alcohol and his eyes were red with fury. A murmuring crowd began to form around them and Tommy knew there would be no reasoning with him. He turned to move back toward Kelly, but Dan quickly stepped in between them.

"Now just hold on," Dan slurred. "I think we need to make things fair. You movin' in on my girl like this, someone's gotta take care of that pretty little thing you probably had to pay."

Dan's *fan club* roared with laughter when he looked to them for approval. Tommy went to sidestep him when suddenly he was shoved to the floor from behind. As he was getting up, Dan grabbed Kelly by the arm and forcefully began to lead her away. His limp did little to slow him down as they made their way to the dance floor. Tommy scrambled to his feet only to get blocked by three of Dan's friends. With a force he had not known he possessed, he shoved through them, knocking two of them to the floor. The third went to reach for him but was stopped short by Riley's tight grip to the collar. As more kids began to join in the tussle, Tommy caught up to Dan and ripped his hand from Kelly's arm. She looked frightened and all Tommy could think of at this moment was to use every ounce of strength in him to slug Dan right in the mouth. He balled his fist and swung hard, blasting him square in his grinning teeth. Dan stumbled backwards and fell to the floor. Blood began to ooze from his lip as he struggled to sit up. Catrina immediately ran to Dan and bent down to tend to him. He shoved her away hard and she fell backwards. The seam on the side of her dress tore and split wide open, exposing a good chunk of her torso. Tommy grabbed Kelly's hand and began to quickly lead her away as faculty came running to assess the disorder. He glanced down at Catrina as they walked past her lying on the floor and he could see pain and desperation in her eyes. He stopped to reach a hand down to help her to her feet. She looked at him apologetically with tears in her eyes as she rose and then at Kelly.

"I'm sorry," she muttered shamefully as she tried to straighten her crumpled, torn dress. Tommy pitifully nodded his head to her and then continued to the exit with Kelly. They paused when they reached the door and waited until the principal, along with a few of the chaperoning teachers, escorted Dan, and his gang out of the gymnasium.

When Tommy was sure they had left the premises, he took Kelly by the hand and led her out the door and down the steps toward his truck.

"Owens!' a voice called from a short distance behind them. He turned to see Sheriff Brady walking briskly towards them.

"Everything okay, Son?" he asked. "Heard there might be some trouble in there?"

Tommy stopped and looked at him, still holding Kelly's hand. "Yes, Sir. We were just leaving. I'm not looking for any trouble."

"I'm sure it was the Rolands boy. Don't worry, I'll have a talk with his father," he said as he continued toward them and then suddenly stopped short when he was able to get a full glimpse of Kelly's face. With a stunned look, he stared hard at her.

"You two get on out of here." he finally said without taking his eyes off her. It made Tommy uneasy, but he was also thankful that he did not ask who she was. He held her hand tighter and led her back to his truck to leave.

It was still early, and Tommy felt horrible that Kelly's night had been ruined.

"I'm sorry," he said when they got in the truck.

"Oh, don't be sorry, Tommy. You were so brave! And I can't wait to tell the children!"

They looked at each other for a second and then burst out laughing at the same time. They knew exactly what their reactions would be. Tommy proceeded to mimic Beth, with wide eyes, a dramatic squeal. And then Billy, with a tough look on his face, *'Bet you got him good!'* Kelly laughed hard at his impressions.

When he finally stopped, he looked at Kelly.

"Hey," he said with a serious expression. "It *is* still pretty early. There's a great big hill that overlooks the world down the road from my house. Maybe we could go there and watch the sunset?"

"The *world*?" she asked, doubtfully.

"The world," he answered boldly, with a big grin.

She looked at him for a moment. Her normal uneasy gut reaction passed rather quickly this time, as she had come to completely trust him. "I would like that," she finally said and smiled. His grin continued as he started the truck and off, they went.

The hill came into sight after traveling a long and winding dirt road about a few miles from Tommy's house. He pulled the truck into a field, turned the engine off, and went around to open the door for Kelly. She slid out of the passenger seat, and he took her hand and then spontaneously began to run full force with her up the big grassy hill. The struggle of trying to keep up with his long strides caused her to laugh loudly, lose her balance, and fall into the grass, pulling him down with her. They both fell and laughed hard. When they finally calmed, they each let out a long breath and just lay there, smiling, and silently taking in the bright blue sky that was scattered with white, fluffy clouds.

"It's so pretty," Kelly finally whispered,

Tommy rolled to his side facing her and propped his head up on one hand to look into her eyes. They seemed to match the sky to perfection. Then he took in every detail of her face. The tiny nose. The glowing skin. The glistening blond hair that laid about her freely in the grass. And the lips. The soft, rose-colored lips. The sight left him breathless.

"Yes, it is," he finally managed, hoarsely. Her sweet scent drew him closer. And then, with such care, he slowly bent his head down to gently place his lips on hers and kissed her. She involuntarily responded and returned the kiss. There was no stopping this reaction. It felt too natural. As he continued to kiss her, she became lost in a feeling she had never experienced. Her mind became dizzy, and her body grew weak and tense all at the same time. The sensation caused her to feel powerless, but she knew she didn't want it to end.

But it did. He pulled away and looked at her. His pupils were dilated, and his face was flush. He looked away and quickly rose to his feet. She lay there confused.

"Are you mad, Tommy?" she asked, worried.

He let out a forced chuckle. "Mad? I assure you I am far from mad." He reached his hand down to pull her to her feet. He cupped her face in his hands. "You make me very happy, Kelly. And that's why it's important that we stop."

She did not know what he meant. But she trusted him. And she loved him. So, she would follow his wishes.

"Come on!" he said, excitedly. "The sun will be setting shortly." He grabbed her hand and once again they were running up the hill. They came to the top and he took his jacket off and laid it on the grass. He guided her to sit with him and together they sat, holding each other, as they watched the sun slowly setting. The colors were glorious. Reds, pinks, and yellows. This day will undoubtedly be the dream, Kelly thought with a smile, which shall top them all.

After a while, Tommy began to sense Kelly's uneasiness. Knowing it had to be the fact that it was almost dark and the risks of sneaking back into the house were getting greater, he stood up and announced that they should be heading home. He pulled her to her feet and placed his hands on her arms. They felt chilled so he briskly rubbed them to warm her before reaching down to grab his jacket and place it around her shoulders.

"Hey," he said, softly, as he reached out to gently sweep her hair out of the jacket and back behind her shoulders. "Thank you for coming with me tonight. I know it is a big risk, and I appreciate it more than you could know." He gently cradled her face with his hands and looked deeply into her eyes. "And I meant what I said, Kelly. I *do* love you."

She intently returned his gaze, and his body shuddered. Her eyes crawled deep into his soul, reaching in, and pulling the strength from his knees. Never had he felt such an intense burning desire as he was feeling now.

He turned his head away to regain his composure before facing her again and then softly placed a gentle kiss on her forehead. But when he stepped back, she grabbed his hands to stop him. She stepped forward and reached up and with her fingertips, slowly traced his jawline and then continued upward to run her fingers through his hair, setting his skin on fire. He closed his eyes and tilted his head sideways to absorb her touch and then reached up to gently take her hand to bring it to his lips and softly kiss it. She lifted her chin and leaned in to boldly place her lips on his and kissed him softly and firmly. He instinctively responded and returned the kiss. While cupping her face once again in his hands, he eagerly traced her lips with his tongue before parting them open to taste every part of her. She responded and shared in this desperate need to explore every inch of him as well until the kiss became so intense and hot, it melted them together as one.

His mind screamed out for him to stop. He did not want to, but he knew that if things went any further, she might end up resenting him. He abruptly stepped back. His breath was heavy, and his head was dizzy.

"Tommy," she said, breathlessly. "What's wrong?"

He took a few deep breaths before answering. "Nothing's wrong," he assured her, tenderly. "We should go."

"Okay," she agreed, confused yet again. "I really do love you."

"I know," he said and smiled sweetly at her before taking her hand to lead her back down the hill towards the truck.

***

The drive back to the house was peaceful. A love song softly played on the radio while Kelly nestled her head against Tommy's shoulder. This night couldn't have ended more perfectly, Tommy thought.

That was until they arrived back at his home. The house was dark, as his parents hadn't arrived home yet, and when he went into the barn to retrieve his four-wheeler to get Kelly home, he discovered somebody had been in there and sliced both back tires flat. He frantically looked around. And it was then that he noticed the deep scrape on the side of Nancy's Camaro door. His blood began to boil.

"*Shit!*" he screamed in anger.

"Tommy?" Kelly asked, nervously.

He looked at her. Although all these discoveries angered him immensely, it was nothing compared to what he felt when he looked at her to see the fear welling up in her eyes.

"Hey," he said and quickly went to her side. "It's okay. I'll get you home. Come on. Let's get back in the truck. "

"You can't," she cried, in a panic.

103

"Kelly, I'll drop you close to your house. I promise he won't see me."

She was in obvious distress, but knowing she had no other choice, she agreed and followed him back to the truck.

As they got close to her home, she let out a sigh of relief. The house was dark. He had not come home yet. She made Tommy stop way before the driveway so that she could get out. She did not kiss him. She did not say goodbye. She just hurriedly got out of the truck.

"Hey!" he yelled before she closed the door. "See you at the creek tomorrow?"

"Okay," she answered quickly, slammed the door, and then rushed off to the back yard.

Tommy pulled away immediately to give her a sense of ease and continued down the road, noting what a deplorable looking shack as he passed what Kelly called home.

As she was scrambling to crawl back through the back basement window in the dark, her arm painfully scraped the side of it causing her to grunt loudly. She quickly got in and held her breath and listened. No sound came from upstairs. All she could hear was the children's gentle breathing. She closed the window and the curtains and quickly went to the secret hiding space and changed into a night shirt. She gently folded the blue dress and put it in the corner with all her favorite things. She left the tiny space and immediately went into the bathroom to scrub the makeup from her face. When she was finished, she crawled onto the mattress next to the children. They were safe and she had made it back unnoticed. Her smile came back, and she could do nothing to erase it from her face as she fell into a slumber of dreams that were filled with Tommy.

CHAPTER 16

Tommy wanted to head back home, but he was too angry. Anger consumed him like never before. One minute he was having the best night of his life, and the next it was completely ruined. Not once, but twice! And all because of *Dan*. He slammed the steering wheel hard with the palm of his hand. Oh, he was gonna make him pay. Dan was gonna pay for Nancy's car *and* the four-wheeler tires. That was for certain. And let's not forget *Father*. How any human being, let alone a father, could instill that much fear in such a sweet, loving girl was unacceptable. Must be a real piece of shit. Both of them. Real pieces of shit. He slammed the steering wheel again.

He continued to drive aimlessly until he reached town. As he was driving past the convenience store, he noticed a group of kids hanging out front. And then he spotted him. Right there in the middle of the group, like a campaigning politician, Dan. Captain Dirt Bag and his brainless army. He slammed on his brakes and then did a complete U-turn. He quickly swung his truck into the store parking lot and squealed to a halt.

The group spread apart to have a look at the aggressive newcomer. Tommy abruptly got out of his truck and slammed the door shut. He strode briskly up to Dan, who had a cigarette dangling from a still swollen lip.

"You're paying for the repairs, you piece of shit," he spat in his face.

"Well," Dan said, sarcastically, looking at Tommy, "Look who's back for more." He then glanced around the group with a wry grin.

"Not only are you paying to get the car *and* my machine fixed, I'm gonna have you charged with trespassing," Tommy continued, angrily.

Dan threw his butt on the ground and grinned again. "Don't know what you're talking about. And trespassing? What do ya own the whole county now? I do a lot of hunting up in those woods by your house. Turkey seasons' startin' soon. They say I'm the best shot around, but hey, ya never know, even the best can have an off day. So, you best watch out for those stray bullets." The group erupted in laughter.

Tommy's blood came to a full boil, and he raised a fist and took a step toward him. "You son of…"

Just then a car squealed in behind them nearly hitting them and halted abruptly. They turned to see Sheriff Brady awkwardly trying to squeeze out of the driver's seat of his cruiser. Dan's group, one by one, began to slither away.

"That'll be enough boys!" he announced and glared at Tommy and Dan.

"Glad you showed up," Tommy said, fuming. "He needs to be arrested! Vandalism and trespassing. Oh, and threatening my life!"

Brady looked hard at Dan and without taking his eyes off him he commanded, "You get on home, Owens. We can take care of this in the morning,"

Tommy glared at him in disbelief. "You heard me," Brady continued as he turned to return the glare. "Best if you went home to cool down." From the corner of his eye, Tommy could see Dan starting to quietly inch away.

"Hold on there, Rolands. Your old man's on the way to pick you up now."

Tommy saw Dan freeze and then ask stiffly. "You called my father?"

"Damn right I did. Looks like him coming around the corner now."

They waited and a few seconds later a white, polished, classic Oldsmobile sporting a gold, naked woman figurine as a hood ornament, pulled into the parking lot. Tommy immediately thought of a pimp car and wanted to laugh but didn't. If anything, it lightened his mood a bit. *What a dick. Must be in the genes.* He watched as a big man, wearing a tall, white, cowboy hat, dug himself out of the car. Two empty beer bottles fell from the car and onto the ground during his struggle. One shattered on the black top and the other just spun around and around until it slowed to a stop. He had on a loud, turquoise button-up-shirt that was partially covered with a black, leather vest that barely fit around his middle.

"Rolands," Brady said and nodded in approval.

"Sheriff," Rolands replied and then looked at Dan, who still had his back to them.

"Get in the car, boy," he said sternly.

Dan turned slowly and without saying a word walked over and got into the passenger side of the *pimp mobile*. Once in the car, he kept his head down, completely defeated. Tommy couldn't help but see him as nothing more than a toddler who got caught with his hand in the cookie jar.

Wow, Tommy thought. *So, this was Oxville law?*

Rolands tipped his hat to Brady, wedged himself back in the car, backed up and drove off.

"Get on home, Owens," Brady reminded Tommy and headed back to his cruiser. Tommy stood there stunned. *Wow. Just wow,* he thought. He watched the white Oldsmobile go two houses down the street and then turn into a driveway. *Too far a pimp to walk?* Tommy thought with sarcastic irony. He got back in his truck and sat for a moment, trying to absorb all that had just happened. Then he backed his truck up, pulled out of the parking lot, and slowly headed down the street toward the Rolands residence with the windows rolled down. As he slowly passed the driveway that he had seen the Oldsmobile pull into, a painful scream brought him to a halt. He pulled over to the curb and sat and listened. And there it was again. A loud, agonizing groan. He turned the engine and lights off and silently sat and continued to listen. Again, the painful scream. He quietly got out of the truck and discreetly walked up the driveway to peer around the back of the house, being extra careful not to get noticed.

To his astonishment, he saw Dan, lying on his back, propped up on one elbow while shielding his face with his free hand. His father towered over him holding a large, heavy, black extension cord. Dan was sobbing loudly and murmuring inaudibly. The once overconfident bully resembled nothing more than a frightened child. Tommy winced as Rolands lifted the chord and forcefully struck Dan across his lifted arm with the cord. The curdling scream came again.

This was too much for Tommy to take. As much as he hated Dan, he could not bear to stand by and watch him get so brutally attacked. Instinctively, he quickly strode up to them and just as Rolands lifted the chord up one more time, Tommy reached up and grabbed it, using all his strength to hold it into place.

Bewildered, Rolands swung around and with wild eyes, shouted. "Who the hell?!"

Tommy held his stance and kept the cord tight in his grip while glaring hard into the assaulter's eyes. After a few seconds, Rolands softened his grip and let the chord fall to the ground.

Dan managed to scramble to his feet and back a few feet away, with his eyes wide with fear. Rolands took his glare off Tommy, turned, and stumbled up the back steps and into the house, letting the screen door slam hard behind him, as though nothing had happened at all.

Tommy looked at Dan with strong concern. He had deep marks on his arms and the shirt he wore was nearly shredded. "Do you want…"

"I'm fine," Dan interrupted, with a shaky voice, refusing to look at him. "You can leave."

"But what if…"

"I said I'm fine, Owens! You can go!" he shouted in anger. But the fear in his eyes told another story when he finally looked at him. "And you best keep your mouth shut about this."

Tommy stood for a moment looking at him helplessly. "I have a spare bedroom if you need a place to crash," he said, sincerely. "You know where I live." And then he reluctantly turned and started back down the driveway, still in shock by what he had just witnessed.

"And Owens!' Dan cried out to him. "I didn't touch your property!" Tommy stopped for a minute but did not turn around. *Bullshit* he thought. But that didn't matter right now. The pity he felt for Dan overpowered anything that he may or may not have done.

As he continued and approached his truck, he suddenly spotted Brady's cruiser also parked alongside the curb. Surely, he must have heard what was going on. Tommy ran up to the car and banged on the window. Without acknowledging Tommy, Brady slowly pulled away from the curb, leaving Tommy standing there, stunned, once again.

CHAPTER 17

The next morning as Kelly busily cut up potatoes and carrots for Father's evening meal, she whistled endlessly the tune, at least what she could remember, that she had heard while dancing with Tommy. She could not wipe the smile from her face even if she tried. And she could not wait to see him later by the creek and maybe feel the softness of his lips again. She stopped herself. *No!* She mustn't think that way. Father would surely say that was a sin and she could not do that again. Seeing Mother again must remain more important than how Tommy made her feel. And it was also for the children.

As she continued to cut up the carrots, the scent caused her mind to drift back to a memory. Mother was in the kitchen at the stove, stirring a big spoon in a large pot of stew. She was humming a pretty tune while Kelly sat at the kitchen table coloring in a book. She would occasionally look at Kelly and smile her beautiful smile. When Kelly was finished with her picture, she carefully tore it from the book and rose to hand it to her. Mother put the large spoon down on the countertop, wiped her hands on her apron, and took the picture from Kelly's hands. She smiled widely and then bent down to wrap her arms around Kelly. Her hands smelled of carrots and onions. The smell she remembered the most. *Beautiful,* she had said. *Just like my little girl.*

But the mood immediately changed as soon as the front door opened. Like it always did. Father stomped into the kitchen like a force and walked over to Mother and roughly pulled her into his arms. He gave her a hard, violent kiss on the lips and Kelly could see Mother shrink back with despise. And this angered him. He shoved her away hard, swung around to the pot of hot stew, and pushed it off the stove top. It went crashing to the floor, splattering hot liquid everywhere. Mother screamed out in pain as it covered both her bare legs. Kelly quickly turned to run to the safety of her bedroom. And the last thing she remembered was turning to glance back to see Mother, who was on all fours, trying to save the picture from the brown liquid that covered the kitchen floor.

She tried to erase these memories from her mind, but they were etched so deeply. The constant and abrupt switch from joy to fear was all that she had known. But with Tommy, it was different. She smiled at herself. It was a wonderful feeling.

She was startled from her thoughts by the sound that she hated more than anything. The sound of the truck pulling into the driveway. *But it was Saturday.* He was usually gone on Friday nights and most of the day on Saturdays. She quickly covered the pot of vegetables, placed it in the refrigerator, and headed to the basement. The children were already huddled on the mattress as they too had become accustomed to the sound of the tires pulling into the drive as an alarm.

After about fifteen minutes, he entered the house. "Where are they?!" he bellowed as he descended the stairs.

They all sat in silent fear.

He marched over to Billy and reached down to grab him by the hair and lifted him to his feet. Billy cried out in pain.

"What have they done?" Kelly asked, fearfully.

Without looking at her, he slowly reached in his pocket and pulled out the watch that Tommy had given her and shoved it into Billy's face for him to see. Her heart stopped. How could she have been so stupid?! In her haste to return home last night she had forgotten all about the watch. It must have come unlatched when she was crawling back through the window. By now her heart was thundering so loud she feared he might hear it.

"Found this outside," he said and squinted around the dark basement suspiciously. "It was right about over there," he said slowly and pointed toward the window that they used to go in and out of. They all froze as he slowly walked to the window and began to inspect it. Suddenly, out of nowhere, Chaz scurried across the floor in front of him, distracting him momentarily. But this time, Father was too quick. His large boot went crashing down on the little animal, creating a faint unsettling popping sound. Billy let out a gasp as he saw Chaz lying flat upon the floor.

Father looked back at him for a moment, unaffected, and then reached up to give the window a shove. It instantly slid open, and he stopped dead.

After a long deafening silence, he finally spoke. "Seems someone broke a lock here," he said with evil glee as if proud of his discovery. He stood for several seconds and stared at it. He seemed to enjoy prolonging the fear that he knew he was surely instilling.

Finally, he spoke. "Kelly, go upstairs."

"Father…" she started.

"Upstairs!" he bellowed like a cannon.

Kelly could see Beth visibly shaking and urine began to run slowly down her leg.

"I broke the lock!" Billy cried out.

Not wanting him to take the punishment, Kelly tried again. "Father…" she cried.

He quickly grabbed Billy by the neck and repeated, calmly this time, "Upstairs." And she knew not to obey would make this much worse. So upstairs she went, fell to the kitchen floor, and cursed herself for what she had done. She should not have taken that watch! She should not have gone to that dance! She should not have kissed Tommy! The tears began to flow. *She should not have kissed Tommy.*

She could now hear Billy shrieking in pain with each strike of the belt. She had figured Father had purposely kept Beth down there to watch just to add to their agony. And as she lay there helplessly shaking on the floor, she thought of Mother. *Mother, this is all for you. Do you really love us?*

When the beating that seemed to last forever ended, she could hear Father come back up the stairs and then out the side door and lock it. And then he was gone.

She wasted no time running down the stairs and to the children. Beth ran to her first and threw her arms around her and buried her head deep into her chest, sobbing uncontrollably.

"Shh…It's okay," Kelly murmured, trying to comfort her. She looked over to see Billy quietly sitting balled up in the far corner, wearing only his underwear. She left Beth's side to go to him and instantly winced at the sight of him. He had welts covering most of his body and some were slowly oozing with blood. She quickly went to grab him a blanket and after draping it around his shoulders, she knelt down beside him and softly stroked his hair. His head was down, and his hands were partially cupped in front of him. She reached down and pulled his hands gently open. Chaz laid there, lifeless, cradled in his palms. He slowly looked up at Kelly and the pain in his eyes was like none she had seen before. But he didn't cry. He *never* cried. She quickly wrapped her arms around him and gently rocked him. He fell limp in her arms and at last, she thought she could hear him sobbing softly. Beth quickly joined them, and she too put her arms around Billy.

"It's gonna be okay," Kelly quietly reassured them. "We're gonna be okay."

But the voice in her mind screamed something else. It was cursing Father at the top of her lungs. They would not be okay. He was probably out buying a new lock. Her world was crumbling.

CHAPTER 18

It was getting to be late in the afternoon and Tommy was still pacing the creek bed waiting for Kelly. She had said she would be there. Just as he was about to give up, Kelly came running breathlessly to him through the woods. The children were not with her.

"Where've you been?" he asked, relieved.

"I can't stay Tommy," she stammered. "I think he went to get a new lock. I'm sorry!"

"What are you talking about?"

"I can't talk now." She turned to leave.

"Kelly! Wait!" he shouted and grabbed her arm. "You can't just run off and leave like this!"

"Tommy, let go!"

"Not until you tell me what's going on!" he insisted. "I want to help!"

She knew she could not tell him everything. There was too much at stake. Desperately she cried, "Leave me alone! I don't need your help! And I don't need you!" And it wasn't until she finally looked away and said, softly, "And I *don't* love you," that he let go of her arm.

The words were like a powerful punch to the gut. "I don't believe you," he finally managed.

Oh, how she wanted to wrap him in her arms and tell him everything. Especially that she did love him. More than anything. But she looked down. "It's true, Tommy. Leave me alone. I really don't love you."

"I don't believe you," he repeated, turning her face to look her into the eyes.

Frustrated, she backed away. "Then you're the stupid one!" she cried and turned to run full speed back into the woods and towards her home.

He stood stunned for a minute before sitting down on a nearby rock and buried his head in his hands. He couldn't believe it. The one person who had come to mean the world to him had let him down. *Let him down?* She literally just tore his heart out. Her bitter words played over and over in his head. He had so many questions. Why didn't the children come? What about a *lock?* The kiss was real. He felt her love. That was real. No, he thought. He did not believe her. He would make her look him straight in the eyes and tell him that she did not love him. This was not over.

He stood up abruptly and took off into the woods where he had seen Kelly disappear. About twenty minutes into his sprint, he spotted a small house. He had to wonder if this was the house he had dropped her at the night before as it looked deserted. The wood siding was weathered and most of the windows were boarded up. It was surrounded by thick trees and sat next to a long, narrow, dirt driveway that ended at a dirt road. He could not see another house in sight from his view, so he reasoned that it had to be the house.

He cautiously went to the back of the house to look into the basement windows. The first window was boarded up, so he continued on to the second window. The ground below this window looked slightly worn and there were no boards so he bent to peer in, but all he could see was darkness. He stood up and walked around to the front of the house and found a front porch. He cautiously climbed the three steps and started to knock on the front door, but instead, stopped short when he found that it was padlocked. It seemed rather stupid. Anybody could easily break the lock to get in. And then panic gripped him. *But what if they wanted to get out?*

Remembering Kelly's mentioning of a lock, he hustled to the back of the house and squatted to look in the second basement window again. He wiped off the dirt with his sleeve to try to get a better look and strained his eyes hard in an attempt to see something in the darkened basement. Just when he thought he might have seen some movement, something cold and hard pressed against the back of his head and he froze.

"You lookin' for something?" a powerful voice said from behind him.

Tommy stayed motionless. There was no question that it was the barrel of a gun pressed against his head.

"Get up, nice and slow," the voice demanded.

Slowly, Tommy rose and turned to see a large, angry looking man holding a rifle. There was something familiar about him, but he couldn't quite put a finger on it.

Then the man formed a wicked, rotten toothed grin and continued, "I shoot trespassers. And ain't nobody gonna find you in these woods."

Tommy panicked, "I…"

"Shut up!" the man bellowed. "Today's your lucky day. Gonna give you to the count of three before I start shooting. One! Two…!"

Tommy was off and running as fast as his legs could take him. The word 'three' rang through the woods and then the shot fired. He ran and ran, his heart racing a mile a minute, until he finally reached his house. Once inside, he slammed the door shut and locked it.

"What in the world?!" a voice called from behind him.

He turned to see his father standing there with his hands on his hips, and a bewildered expression on his face. Fighting to catch his breath, Tommy stammered, "There's a man trying to shoot me!"

"What?!" Pete yelled, astonished.

"Back in the woods," Tommy continued, in between breaths. "I think he has Kelly and the kids locked up!"

"What?" Nancy exclaimed as she walked into the room.

Tommy proceeded to explain his suspicions when Pete held his hand up to stop him. "Hang on, Tom. These farmers around here are pretty protective of their property. And that's an awfully big accusation. I don't know what you're getting yourself into, but if this girl is filling your head with crazy notions, you best take a step back."

Before Tommy had the chance to argue his point, Nancy cut in and firmly stated, "I believe him."

Pete looked at her and sighed. "Okay," he said. He turned his attention back to Tommy. "If the girl didn't come right out and tell you what you suspect, it's gonna be tough to get her help. And back to the subject of property, what in the hell happened to your mother's car?!"

Tommy's shoulders dropped. "I don't know, Dad. My four-wheeler tires got sliced, too."

"You don't know who would have done this?" he asked, with annoyance.

Tommy shook his head no.

"Well, so much for a *safe, little, town*. Apparently, there's a vandal out there. I'm gonna call the Sheriff and take care of all of this. Hopefully, he can get to the bottom of it. In the meantime, we need to start locking the barn door *and* you need to stay away from that house."

***

That night Tommy tossed and turned. He couldn't get the man who pressed the gun against his head out of his mind. Or Kelly's angry words. She would never have said those awful things and that scared him even more. And then a more frightening thought crossed his mind. *Perhaps there was a barrel against Kelly's head as well.*

CHAPTER 19

Father went down the basement stairs with the rifle and stared at Kelly.

"Light the candle," he ordered. The tone of his voice meant punishment was coming.

She reached for the matches and dropped them three times as her hands shook with fear. The children quickly huddled together on the mattress.

"You're just like your Momma, afterall," he said with an eerie confidence and then spat on her. She did not budge to wipe it off.

"Meeting with boys outside to pleasure yourself."

"No, Father…" she desperately began.

"Shut up!" He commanded and swiftly swung the gun's barrel across her face causing her to yell out in pain and fall hard onto the floor. Her lip was split open and began to ooze with blood.

Billy jumped to his feet and yelled, "Stop!"

Father kicked his foot out into his stomach causing him to tumble backwards onto the mattress.

"Your sister sinned!" he roared. "If you don't stay out of this, ain't none of you gonna see your Momma tomorrow!"

They all looked at him in silent disbelief.

"That's right," he snickered. "You're gonna go see your Momma tomorrow."

Kelly could see joy begin to replace the children's fear. *Could this be true? Finally true?"*

"First," he said, interrupting their hopes. "I got to cleanse your sister of her sins."

He looked long and hard at her. He never stared directly into her eyes, and now that he was, it sickened her. The ugliness that poured from his angry, bulging eyes seemed to seep deep into her soul, poisoning her from the inside out. Without taking his eyes from her, he finally commanded the children, "Go get in that room."

They stood motionless and looked at him in shock. *He knew about the room!*

"Get!" he shouted.

They scrambled to their feet and ran to move the piece of plywood that blocked the entrance to the secret room and quickly climbed in.

He broke his stare and slowly walked over to move the plywood back into place and then turned back to Kelly.

"You wanna act like you're Momma," he said to her, "Then I'm gonna treat you like your Momma. Get yourself undressed."

She stood there scared and confused, unbudging. *What was happening?* He waited a few more minutes, and then as if something snapped inside of him, he angrily sprang to her and grabbed her hard by the throat with both hands, causing her to choke and fight for air. The awful stench that his breath carried when he was at his worst filled her nostrils. She desperately tried to pull her neck free from his grip while grasping at his hands, but he squeezed even harder until she could feel herself become dizzy. Mother entered her mind, and the gruesome scene quickly appeared as well.

"Please stop!" Mother cried as he reached for her throat. Her arms frailed and her feet kicked as he ripped the nightgown from her body with his free hand. She turned her head to the side and Kelly, who was lying nearby on the floor with a coloring book, could see the desperation in her eyes as she lay helpless with him towering over her with his massive body.

The vision snapped from Kelly's mind when she felt his hands release her neck. But it wasn't over. In a continued rage, he quickly tugged at her own dress and the rest became a big blur. She could feel his hands hard all over her body and then a pain so unbearable seared through her insides that it caused her to vomit. And he got angrier, so it became more painful until she finally became numb. No thoughts, nor prayers, filled her mind. Completely lost, she let go and escaped from her body and into darkness.

CHAPTER 20

Monday morning had come, and Tommy was reluctantly sitting in his first period English class. He could not concentrate on his teacher's words or the lesson she was teaching. Too many things were going through his mind. His fear for Kelly and the kids was growing by the minute and he still refused to believe that the cruel words she had spoken to him had come from her heart.

And then there was Dan. He had come into class late. He quickly glanced at Tommy with embarrassment and then looked away. He humbly sat down and quietly opened his book. No threatening glares. No demeaning remarks. Everything seemed off and unsettled. So, when the bell rang to end the period, Tommy headed straight for the door with the full intention of skipping the rest of the school day.

***

Tommy got home and headed straight to the barn to retrieve his four-wheeler.

"Tommy?!" he heard his mother yell as she came off the front steps, wiping her hands on her apron. "What are you doing at home? Is everything okay?"

"Yea, Mom," he answered back, impatiently. "Just wasn't feeling good today."

"Well, come inside. I'll fix you some tea," she pleaded.

"I'm okay, Mom. Just want to take a little ride."

Before she could persuade him further, he had started the four-wheeler and was off heading into the woods. When Kelly's house came into sight, he pulled his machine around to the side and slid off. The driveway was empty, and the padlock was on the front door again, so he went around the back to the basement window and looked in. This time he was sure of what he saw. It was Beth. She looked up at him and stopped short. Then Billy came to the window.

"Let me in!" Tommy called.

"I can't!" Billy called back. "It's locked!"

Tommy looked around desperately. He noticed a shovel leaning against a tree a few yards away. Thanking his luck, he briskly walked over to retrieve it.

"Stand back!" he yelled when he returned to the window, and then with a swift and forceful swing, he struck the window hard and watched it shatter. He pulled his sleeve over his hand and began to knock the remaining glass away so that he could crawl in. The children stood horrified.

The stench of septic hit him immediately. He turned up his nose and grimaced as he glanced around the basement. Even though the lighting was close to dark, he could see the mattresses lying on the floor. Puzzled, he turned to the children.

"Where's Kelly?" he demanded.

Beth pointed to a corner in the far side of the basement behind the clothesline. He cautiously made his way over, ducked his head under the clothes, and squinted to find her. There she sat, with her head buried in her arms, not moving.

"She won't talk to us," Beth said sadly, as she crept up behind him. "We're gonna see Mother today and Kelly can't even talk."

Tommy rushed to Kelly's side and bent down beside her. Even in the darkness, he could see the bruises on her neck and arms and the blood stains on her dress.

"My God," he groaned. "What happened?"

Kelly would not look at him.

"Father did it," Beth answered for her. "And now she won't talk."

"Okay," he replied, sullenly and looked back at the children. "Get yourselves together. I'm getting you out of here."

They looked at Kelly, but she did not budge. Tommy bent down impatiently to lift her off the floor when she shouted, "No!"

He stared at her for a moment, and she repeated, softly, "No."

"Kelly," Tommy said, relieved to hear her speak, "You can't live like this any longer. It's wrong. My God, it's against the law in the least!"

"No," she said again and looked at him this time.

"But what your father is doing…"

"It was my fault," she cut in. "I paid for my sins. I should have never kissed you."

He looked at her astonished. "I kissed you because I love you," he said desperately. "That is *not* a sin."

She looked at him and tears began to form. "I…I don't know why he did that to me." She began to tremble and then the tears began to flow more steadily from her eyes. He quickly knelt down beside her and wrapped an arm around her.

"Tommy," she said between sniffles, "I want to be with you. And to be safe. But I've waited a long, long time to see Mother."

"Exactly how long have you waited?" he asked with bewilderment.

Kelly looked away and stared at the broken window. "I know I was six. And I think I am sixteen now. I've been watching Father's calendars. So…"

"Ten years," he said, pathetically, and shook his head. "And the kids?"

"Beth was a baby, but Billy was a brand-new baby when Mother left. I have been taking care of them."

"She left you with *babies*? "

She looked at them and nodded. "Yes. But things got way better when the lock broke."

He sat in disbelief for a moment trying to absorb all that she had told him.

"How are you sure about your mother?" he asked.

"The letters," she answered, eagerly. "I saved them all.

"She sends you letters? How did you know what they said?"

"Because Father tells…" she began and then stopped short and looked at him with panic in her eyes.

His shoulders dropped and he sighed loudly. "Bring me the letters," he gently urged her.

She stood up and slowly walked to the secret room, stopping a few times to wince in pain, and returned with the neatly stacked pile of letters and handed them to him. He glanced around the basement with disgust once again before taking the letters from her. He proceeded to leaf through the pile before retrieving one to open. He scanned it quickly with his eyes and then looked up at her. "What is your mother's name?"

"Camille," she said, and managed a slight smile. "It's a very pretty name. Just like her. Camille Johnson."

Kelly suddenly grabbed the letter from his hands with excitement. *She could almost* read *now. Why did she not think of this sooner?* As she began to sound out the words, she quickly became confused. Mother did not start with a *C*. Was Camile a *C* or a *K*? She looked up at Tommy in desperation. He gently took the letter back and slowly shook his head.

"This letter is from someone named Carol. Made out to Charles. Is that your father's name?"

She slowly shook her head yes, feeling her world sinking.

"She's begging him to bring the children back. Do you know who she might be?" he asked.

"I had an Aunt Carol, I think. I don't really remember much about her, though," she replied.

He looked again at the letter. "Canidy. Does that sound familiar?" he asked.

"I lived there!" she proclaimed. "I know that name! There was a big park there with swings and lots of flowers! Me, Mother, Beth, and Chris would go there!"

"Who is Chris?" he asked.

"Mother's friend. *And* mine. He was very nice, and I really liked him. He would bring me ice cream and candies sometimes." she said and smiled again.

"What else do you remember about him?" he urged.

She thought hard. "Um…well he had a dog! A dog with floppy ears and we would take turns throwing a ball to him." She paused and thought some more. "Oh, and he wore a white coat sometimes."

"You mean like a doctor?" Tommy asked.

She shrugged her shoulders. "I don't know."

"Of course, you wouldn't," he replied and put his head down, absorbed in thought.

"If Carol knew you were here, why wouldn't she come for you?" he quietly asked himself. And then he shook his head in dismay and answered his own question. "Because she didn't know you were here."

He looked back at Kelly. "I'm guessing these letters were forwarded. Did you save the envelopes?"

"No," she answered, helplessly.

"It's okay. Look, I'm gonna help you guys, but you can't stay here. Especially with the window broken. It's even more dangerous now. I want you to come home with me."

A look of panic crossed her face. "Please, Tommy. Just one more day. If Mother really is coming, I need to see her!" she pleaded. "I will keep the curtain on the window closed."

"Please, Tommy!" Beth begged. "I want to see our mother!"

"If we don't see her by tomorrow, we will leave with you," Kelly promised. "But you must leave now. If Father comes home and finds you here, you will ruin it for all of us!"

Tommy was torn. He did not want to leave without them, but Kelly was too persistent. He walked over to the window, took his hoodie off to create a makeshift sack, and proceeded to place the broken glass in it.

"Make sure you close these curtains," he ordered the children when he finished and then reluctantly headed back out the window with the glass in tow. He jumped on his four-wheeler and headed back through the woods.

***

Pete was waiting for him when he returned home.

"I had a feeling you left school today," he said sternly, as Tommy entered the house. "And your mother verified it for me."

"Dad, wait," he stammered. "It's true. They *are* being held captive and abused. Just as I thought. We need to help them. Kelly claims they are waiting for their mother, but I don't trust that son-of-a-bitch!"

Pete raised his eyebrows at his son's choice of uncharacteristic words before continuing, "You've seen for yourself?"

"Yes, Dad! It's horrible! I can't even begin to tell you how bad it is."

"Okay, Tom. Get in the car. We're going to the Sheriff's office."

Tommy hesitated. "We can't Dad. I promised I'd give her one more day. She claims her mother is coming for them. And if we interfere, we'll ruin it."

Pete looked at him skeptically. "And do you believe this?"

"I believe her," he said quietly and looked down. "I just don't believe him," he continued and looked up worried.

"Then we better get them some help," Pete said, and reached for his coat." We will find this mother once they are safe."

123

When they arrived at the police station, Sheriff Brady was sitting at a desk with his feet propped up, finishing the last bite of a donut.

"Well, Mr. Owens. Was wondering when I might see you again," he said as he stood up and wiped his hands on his pants. "Been checking around on that vandalism incident. Gonna stop by the Rolands' later today. Guessin' his boy might have had something to do with it." He shot Tommy a knowing look.

"It wasn't Rolands," Tommy stated, returning a more hostile look. Although he was almost certain that it probably was, he couldn't bear the thought of being responsible for a repeat attack like the one he had witnessed the other night. And how Brady could have allowed that to happen still baffled him. Brady sneered at Tommy and then returned his attention to Pete. "Well, I'll certainly try to get to the bottom of it. In the meantime, it wouldn't hurt to put a call into your insurance company."

"I plan on it," Pete responded. "But I'm afraid we're here for another reason."

"You folks care for a doughnut?" Brady asked, uninterested, and held up a box of peanut coated fry cakes.

Tommy cut in, impatiently, "Do you know there's a man in this town holding his own children captive? Abusing them? They are living worse than animals!"

"Whoa!" Sheriff Brady said as he wiped the crumbs from his mouth. "Calm down, Son. What is it that you think you know?"

Tommy told him everything that he had witnessed, including getting shot at.

"We need to get there and save them!" he demanded when he finished.

"Johnson, huh?" Sheriff Brady pondered. "He's a mechanic down at the sawmill. Not the most pleasant guy, but never really bothers anybody. Just a bar fight now and again. I *do* know that he doesn't have any kids. Nor a wife for that matter. But you say you saw these things? And were shot at?" He paused for a moment. "Sure you're not still mad at the fender bender? Seems you've been in the middle of a lot of trouble lately."

Pete looked at Tommy, quizzically.

"You're kidding?" Tommy asked with disgust, ignoring his father's look.

Brady looked at Pete and raised his eyebrows.

"Watch your tone, son," Pete warned.

"I'll swing by today and have a talk with him," Brady finally replied, seemingly satisfied with Pete's interference as he began picking the crumbs out of his teeth with his pinky fingernail. Tommy could tell he was not buying his story. "Can we please go now? I'm afraid for their lives," he insisted with desperation.

Brady impatiently sighed and then slowly walked into another room and closed the door. After a few minutes he returned wearing his coat and campaign hat. "I'll check it out now," he said, flatly, and the three of them walked out the door.

"We're gonna follow you," Tommy announced and looked at Pete pressingly.

"Whatever you gotta do," Brady replied, dully.

***

They pulled into the dirt driveway of Charlie Johnson's and parked behind his truck. Sheriff Brady got out and walked up the front steps with Pete and Tommy behind him. After five knocks, Sheriff Brady sighed and turned around and shrugged. Just then the door opened.

"Sheriff?" came the deep growl of Charlie Johnson as he stood towering in the doorway.

"Uh, Charlie," Sheriff Brady started, appearing embarrassed. "We have a bit of a problem. This young man here claims you shot at him?"

Charlie said nothing.

"And," Brady continued, "Thinks you may have some children in your basement?"

Charlie let out a deep, short grunt and glared at Tommy. "Is that right?"

"If we can just take a look around, just to clear this up, we can put this to rest."

"Well," Charlie said, after a moment. "The law says you need a search warrant."

"Fair enough," Brady agreed and turned to Pete and Tommy and shrugged his shoulders once again. "That'll take some time."

125

"But," Charlie continued, "I got nothing to hide, so go ahead and take a look if you have to." He stepped aside so that Brady and Pete could enter the house but moved to deliberately block Tommy's entrance. "You ain't welcome," he stated, flatly.

Sheriff Brady motioned for Tommy to wait outside. As he and Pete entered the house, Tommy yelled in a panic, "Make sure you check the basement wall!"

Charlie turned to Tommy before he shut the door and gave him an eerie grin and then winked at him. Blood boiled deep in Tommy, and he did all he could to keep from charging past him and through the door.

After Tommy paced in the driveway for what seemed much too short for a search, the three came back out of the house.

"Sorry, Charlie," Brady said, apologetically.

In utter disbelief, Tommy glared at his dad for answers.

"There's nothing here," Pete told him.

"No!" Tommy yelled. "You didn't look good enough! You didn't look in the basement!"

"We did…" Pete started.

"No!" Tommy continued, in a panic. "You didn't check the hiding place!" He forcefully pushed through his father and the sheriff but was stopped abruptly when Charlie reached out and grabbed him by the arm with such a fierce grip, it caused Tommy to wince in pain.

"Not too late for me to press trespassing charges on you, boy," Charlie said with an eerie calm.

"Okay," Sheriff Brady cut in, impatiently, "No need for charges. Owens, get your boy under control."

"Let's go Tom," Pete commanded.

"Dad!" Tommy pleaded, as he broke free from Charlie's grip, "They're here. I know it! You didn't look hard enough!"

He once again went to go up the stairs when Pete grabbed his arm this time and shouted, "Tom, enough! We're leaving."

As Pete and Tommy drove away, Tommy turned to glance back at the house one last time. Sheriff Brady was shouting angrily at Johnson. *Where was this five minutes ago?* Nothing made sense. And there was no point in mentioning this to Pete. The look on his face told him that he had reached his limit. So, Tommy sat with silent anger for the entire ride back home. *How could they not find anything?* Tommy thought.

What about the mattresses? Kelly and the children will no doubt pay for this, and he must come up with a plan to help them.

When they arrived home, Pete put the car in park and sat for a minute before turning to look boldly at Tommy. He let out a sigh of disgust and then finally spoke, "Those children that you have been spending time with obviously do not live there."

"Dad," Tommy began desperately, but was cut short when Pete continued, more loudly, "And it appears that your friend, the young lady, may not be being completely honest with you. You will not do anything that will get you in trouble with the law."

Tommy's blood continued to boil. "I don't care about the law! I care about…"

"*AND!*" Pete continued, talking even louder over him," I will be looking to book us a flight to Chicago for the morning. We can spend a few days there. I think we can all use a little time away to catch up with some old friends. It'll do us good. *Especially* you."

No, *WE are not,* Tommy thought, as he hastily got out of the car, went into the house and stormed up the stairs to his bedroom, slamming the door hard behind him. *NO, WE ARE NOT.*

CHAPTER 21

Kelly could hardly breathe. The newly discovered space deep inside the hiding spot was dark and cold, but more than anything, small. It branched off from their regular hiding spot, buried deep inside the wall, connected only by a crawl space that's opening was covered by a painting splashed with random colors. Kelly did not know about this extra space, but apparently, Father did. And as she sat cramped in the corner of this tiny space, she had to wonder how long he knew about their space with all their special things and if they would be punished for it.

The children were extra quiet during the search. This was their last test, and they were sure that they had passed.

"They didn't find us," Billy whispered. "We're gonna see Mother!"

"Shhh…" Kelly whispered.

She could hear footsteps coming down the stairs and then the plywood being pushed aside.

"Get on out of there!" Father's boisterous voice demanded.

They pushed the painting aside and then scurried from the hiding spot like rats, gasping for air. As they lined up in front of him waiting for his next command, Kelly secretly scanned the basement. She could see the clothes that she had recently hand washed and hung on the clothesline, clumped on the floor in the corner and the mattresses that they slept on, stacked and leaning against a wall.

He looked at them and shook his head with approval.

"Good," he stated. "You all done well." And then he turned to Kelly. "Your boyfriend there…not done with him." He then let out a cruel laugh. "Gonna teach him a lesson for sticking his nose where it don't belong. Stupid boy!"

"Tommy's not stupid!" Beth quickly cried out, with uncharacterized confidence.

Kelly's stomach grew hard. God, she wished Beth hadn't said that. But she knew Tommy had come to mean so much to them. Just as he did to her.

He looked quizzically at Beth. "He's *your* boyfriend too?" he asked.

Beth looked back at him with anger in her eyes.

"Hmm..." he grunted, as he reached down to her and slowly began to stroke her hair. She winced and closed her eyes but did not move.

"Don't," Kelly said, sternly.

He turned to look at her comically. "Don't? Don't or what?"

Kelly looked boldly in his eyes and replied flatly, "I'll kill you."

A look of shock crossed his face before a loud sickening laugh exploded from his mouth. It sent shivers down her body, but she continued to hold her stance.

"And do you think your Momma's gonna wanna visit you in jail?" he asked, comically. "Do ya? She won't go visit sinners."

"Leave Beth alone, or I will kill you," she repeated, unaffected by his threat.

He stared at her long and hard, but she stared back just as hard and held her ground. She could sense an uneasiness growing in him. She had never stood up to him like this before and she could tell it was making him uncomfortable. It was he who finally broke the staredown. He turned, walked across the basement, and stomped back up the stairs. Kelly let out a sigh of relief as the children ran to wrap their arms around her. She knew what she did might have risked everything, but she would not let him hurt Beth the way that he had hurt her. She would fight him to the death before she would ever let that happen.

But it wasn't long before he stomped back down the stairs. Only this time, to her horror, he was carrying a rifle. *What had she done?!*

As he approached her, she grabbed the children by the arms and cautiously backed them away with her. He slowly lifted the rifle when he reached her and just as she was about to drop to her knees and beg for mercy, he extended his arms and offered it to her instead.

"Here," he said, and shifted the rifle closer to her.

She stood confused for a moment and then with trembling hands, reached out to take it from his hands.

"Go ahead," he continued, with eerie calmness. "Go ahead and kill me."

When she didn't budge, he erupted in laughter.

"Just what I thought," he spat. "You ain't got it in ya!"

He reached out again to boldly stroke Beth's hair and with a smug expression on his face, glanced back at Kelly. But instead of the frightened reaction he was expecting to find, he was stopped short by the sound of the click of the trigger. A deafening silence filled the basement as Kelly stood, visibly shaking, with one finger on the rifle's trigger while she pointed the barrel directly at his chest.

He widened his eyes in surprise and then smiled wryly.

"Would you look at that?" he mused.

As he slowly reached out to take the rifle back from her, she squeezed the trigger again. And again, it did not fire. She quickly squeezed the trigger one more time and still nothing happened.

She stood in shock as he snatched the gun from her hands and then stared at her with surprise, as if almost proud of her. She quickly turned away from him and a whirlwind of emotions exploded in her head. Anger, fear, and relief. *If the gun had fired, would God have forgiven her?* Seeming pleased with her anguish, he turned to make his way back to the stairs. When he reached the top step, he yelled back down to them, "Get some rest! You're gonna see your Momma tonight!"

Kelly, Beth, and Billy all froze and looked at each other in disbelief. They stood silent for a moment before rushing in to squeeze each other long and hard. Kelly took a step back and looked at the children with tears in her eyes and a smile on her face. The encounter with Father was quickly gone from her mind and replaced with incredible joy. The time had come. *The time had finally come.*

CHAPTER 22

Tommy knew that the broken window would no doubt cause great harm to Kelly and the kids, so he wasted no time locating a directory for Canidy. Unfortunately, the town was about two hours away. He searched thoroughly but could not find a listing for Carol Johnson.

He sat and thought hard. And then Mr. Bradshaw came to mind. Surely, he would know something. He ran to the kitchen 'junk drawer' and began to frantically rummage through the random notes and papers that Nancy would throw in there. And after digging for about five minutes, he found Harry Bradshaw's phone number scribbled on a small piece of paper. He dialed the number and after three rings, a woman's voice answered.

"Hello?"

"Um…can I speak with Mr. Bradshaw?" he asked, awkwardly.

"Who is this?" the woman asked, slightly annoyed.

"This is Tommy Owens. I live in his old house in Oxville. It's important that I talk to him."

There was a moment of silence before the woman finally answered.

"Owens. Yes, I know the name. This is Harry's daughter, Lucy. I'm afraid my father is not doing very well. What is it that you need?"

Not sure how to approach the subject, Tommy continued cautiously, "There is a man that lives a couple of miles from here. Out behind the woods. The name is Johnson. I need information about him. Specifically, proof that he has children. I feel…, no I mean I *know*, they are in great danger."

"Johnson," the woman repeated. "Yeah, I know who you mean. We were warned to stay away from him. Not sure about children though. Rumor was his father, a preacher, died in jail. Murdered his mother, I guess."

Tommy's heart sank. "And you don't know anything about a wife or kids?"

"No, I'm sorry," she answered, sincerely. "Perhaps you should call the police?"

"Brady wasn't any help."

"Well, that doesn't surprise me," she said, wryly, "He was the one who warned us."

Tommy grunted, hopelessly. "Well, sorry to hear about your dad. If you can, tell him we wish him well."

"Thank you, I will. I'm afraid his mind has gone downhill rather fast. He sleeps all day and stays awake most of the night. He seems completely lost and confused these days. We're doing our best just to keep him comfortable."

Just then Tommy could hear a voice rumbling in the background through the phone. "It's okay, Dad," he heard Lucy say to the voice. "Go on back to bed. I'll be there in a minute." She returned her attention back to Tommy. "Sorry. I'm afraid any conversation with you would only confuse him."

"I understand," he assured her.

He hung up the phone, feeling lost. He had to do something. And then he remembered the doctor that Kelly had spoken of. *Dr. Chris!* His heart raced as he quickly scanned through the Physicians section in the directory. *Bingo!* Dr. Chris Sperling, M.D. He dialed the number and waited for an answer. It rang and rang until an answering machine finally came on. *"You have reached Dr. Sperling. If this is an emergency, hang up and dial 911. Business hours are from 8 a.m. to 5 p.m. Monday through Friday. If you are calling after hours, please leave a message."* He looked at the clock, cursed, and hung up. It was going on six o'clock. They were gone for the day. Well, he decided he would not wait another day to try everything he could to save Kelly and the children. He quickly jotted the address down.

He waited until seven o'clock. That was the time his parents usually retired to the back enclosed sunroom to share an after-dinner glass of wine and watch the evening news. He tipped-toed into the kitchen and grabbed his truck keys. They may or may not hear him sneak off now, but they would surely notice him gone later that night. And they will be furious. But that was the chance he was willing to take. There was no way they would give him permission, so he would have to just go without it.

***

Tommy reached the small town of Canidy a little after nine and he quickly found the doctor's office. It was located on a well-manicured cul-de-sac and, much to his relief, looked as though it was attached to

134

a residence. He circled around and pulled into the drive. The lights were still on inside the house, so he got out of his truck and walked up the sidewalk to knock on the front door. When the door finally opened, a short, elderly man wearing wire rimmed glasses and a plaid housecoat stood there.

"I need to speak to you," Tommy stated, desperately, before the man even had a chance to speak. "It's about Kelly Johnson."

The man stared at him with confusion before finally speaking. "Is she a patient?"

"No! Well, not anymore. Don't you remember her? Her mother's name is Camille."

He thought for a moment and then a look of remembrance crossed his face.

"Ah, yes, Camille. A face not easy to forget," he said as his eyes lit up. "Haven't seen them in many years. What is it that you want from me?"

"They need help. I was hoping you could help me. Apparently, you used to spend time with them."

The doctor looked taken aback. "The only time I saw them was for a check up here and there. Not sure how that helps."

"Kelly said she used to spend time with a doctor. A doctor Chris. It has to be you."

A look of confusion crossed his face again and he shook his head. "I'm sorry. I don't recall spending any time with them other than an occasional office visit."

Tommy painfully stared at him for a moment and then, feeling defeated, turned to leave. "Sorry to have bothered you," he managed as he headed back towards his truck.

"Hey!" yelled the doctor as Tommy was about to get in his truck. "What about Chris Crawford?! He's the vet in town!"

Tommy stopped and looked back at him with a glimpse of hope. *It made sense. Veterinarians could wear white coats, too.* He quickly trotted back to the house. "Do you know how I can find him?"

"His office is just outside of town, but I'm sure he's gone at this hour. He lives on Meyer Street. Just take a left at the light in town. It's the big white house about a mile down the road on the left. His mailbox is in the shape of a dog," he said, comically, "You can't miss it."

The vet's house was easy enough to find. Unfortunately, there were no lights on inside. Still, he wasted no time pulling into the driveway and rushing to the front door to ring the doorbell. He could hear a dog barking, insistently, inside. It wasn't until he pushed the doorbell a third time that a light came on from inside.

The door opened and a tall, distinguished looking man with wavy, chestnut hair stood there in a housecoat.

"Chris?" Tommy asked, with a last shred of hope.

"Yes?" the man answered, suspiciously, as he turned to calm the dog that seemed overly anxious to meet this new stranger.

"I need your help. I have a friend who I believe is in grave danger," he gushed.

"I'm a vet," Chris replied, and waved his arms in the air quizzically.

"I know," Tommy continued. "This is about a girl and her siblings. Kelly Johnson. Do you remember her?"

Chris's jaw immediately dropped, and his face turned white.

"Come in," he finally managed, softly.

Tommy followed him through the foyer and into the kitchen, stopping every few steps to pet the dog that was jumping on his leg begging for his attention.

"Max, down!" Chris commanded the dog and then motioned for Tommy to sit in a chair at the kitchen table. He then walked to the counter and proceeded to gather supplies to make a pot of coffee.

"Would you like coffee?" he asked Tommy as he poured the water from the carafe into the top of the coffee maker.

"No, sir," Tommy answered. "Something is telling me I don't have a lot of time."

Chris was about to speak when a tall woman, with long, blond curls, wearing a plush pink robe, walked into the kitchen.

"Is everything ok?" she asked.

Tommy looked at her. Kelly's description fit her to a tee. He stood up abruptly and glared at her.

"*Is everything ok*?" he snarled. "Are you kidding me?! I'm here trying to save Kelly, Beth, and Billy! Tell me you're not so heartless that you don't remember who they are!"

"Hold on!" Chris snapped. "Who are you?!"

Tommy took a deep breath and returned his attention to Chris.

"My name's Tommy Owens. I've been spending a lot of time with *her* children, and I came here because they are in grave danger from their father."

Chris shook his head in disbelief and then calmly said, "This is my wife, JoAnne. This is not Camille. Camille left town years ago with her kids and that son-of-a-bitch she was married to. I tried for a *long* time to track her down, but I couldn't find her." He took a deep breath and sat down and motioned for Tommy to join him.

"You've been in touch with little Kelly Johnson?" he asked, with hope in his voice.

"Yeah, I've been *more* than in touch. She's become the most important part of my life, and she means the world to me. And so do the kids."

"The kids?" Chris asked, confused. "You mean Beth."

"Billy and Beth."

Chris's eyes widened. "Who is Billy?"

"Her younger brother," he answered.

"How old?" Chris asked, with desperation.

"Ten, I think," Tommy answered, finding the line of questioning irritating considering the desperate circumstances.

"You think?" he asked, confused.

"They're being held captive by their psycho father. I think for the past ten years. Billy was a newborn. Kelly's been raising them both."

"My God," Chris sighed. "And Camille is not with them?"

"No, but the old man claims she is supposed to meet back up with them tonight after all these years. They have been living in hell. And I don't trust that he is telling them the truth. I promise you. They are in danger."

Chris put his elbows on the table and placed his head in his hands.

"Chris?" JoAnne asked, concerned as she placed a cup of coffee in front of him.

He slowly looked up at her and said, with grave certainty, "The boy. He's my son."

"What are you saying?" Tommy probed.

Chris let out a long sigh. "It happened so long ago, but it feels like yesterday," he started, as if in a daze. "It wasn't long after I met Camille that I realized she was in an abusive marriage. Charlie was a bastard, the way he treated her. She was scared to death of him." He shook his head and continued, "Anyway, it took some time but she came to finally trust me. And confide in me." He looked at JoAnne, sorrowfully, and then back to Tommy. "She was forced into that marriage. She tried to end it with him when they were dating, but she got pregnant when he forced himself on her. Things were different back then. Her parents didn't help or listen to her fears." He paused to take a sip of his coffee. "Anyway, we became very close, and it didn't take long for me to fall deeply in love with her. I loved Kelly. And I loved Beth." He stopped and smiled sadly as he remembered them. "The last time I saw her we had met at the park where we spent a lot of time together. She looked like she had just gone ten rounds in a cage fight. Her eyes were black. She had bruises everywhere. I was livid! I was gonna tear straight to her house and kill that son-of-a-bitch!" He paused for a few seconds to compose himself and to give JoAnne a reassuring glance. "But she stopped me," he continued. "She promised me she would take Kelly and Beth and finally leave him. Just one more day is all she needed. She had a few more things to take care of."

Tommy took a sharp breath in. *Just one more day.* Those were Kelly's words as well.

Chris shook his head again in disgust before continuing, "And then the bombshell. She told me that she was pregnant and was certain that I was the father! I was over the moon! There was *no* way in hell I was gonna allow him to put one more finger on her. Especially with her carrying *my* child! Oh, I begged her not to go back. Not even for one more day. But she insisted. So, the plan was for her to meet me back there the following day so that we could leave town and begin our lives together. She promised me that he wouldn't be home for a couple days." He paused as a tear formed in his eye. "But she never showed. I waited longer than I should have and finally went to that shit hole she called home, and it was empty. Gone. They all disappeared into thin air."

Tommy sat filled with emotion. Kelly remembered the park memories. They were probably the last beautiful moments she had with her mother.

"Did you call the police?" JoAnne asked.

"I did," Tommy replied. "But the old man hid them, so the police don't believe me. And now after talking to you," he said, returning his attention to Chris, "And getting the whole story, I'm convinced something bad *will* happen and I have to stop it." He stood up.

Chris followed suit. "I'm going with you," he said, with resolution.

He turned to JoAnne and with a look of desperation, announced, "I have to go."

She walked over to him, wrapped her arms around him and hugged him tightly. Then she looked up at him and softly said, "I know. Go help those children."

After a quick change of clothes for Chris, he and Tommy were on their way to Oxville.

CHAPTER 23

It was deep in the night and Father, with a sack slung over his shoulder and a lantern dangling from one hand, began the trek through the woods with the children to finally meet Mother. He had woken them in their sleep, so Kelly had no idea what the time was, but it didn't matter. She felt more alert than ever. The kids had a skip to their gait and Kelly could tell they were excited. Even the walk with Father did not frighten them. She smiled. It was here. It was *finally* here. She would throw her arms around Mother and never let go. And this gave her courage. Courage to ask Father questions.

"Is Mother in the woods?" she asked.

"Yep," he answered. "She'll get here. Don't need the neighbors seeing everything going on."

"How much further?" she asked after fifteen more minutes of walking.

"Almost there," he grumbled.

When he finally stopped them, they were deep in the woods. He hung the lantern on a tree branch and sat down on a log.

"Where is she?" Kelly asked.

"You'll see her." he answered dully, as if in deep thought.

Kelly, Beth, and Billy also found a large tree log to rest on. The children carried on about how pretty and nice their mother was gonna be. They took turns practicing what they would say to her.

But as the minutes passed, Kelly began to become unnerved. It was starting to not make sense. Why would he make Mother meet them in the woods? What if she didn't have a lantern? Just as she was about to voice her concerns, she noticed the rifle leaning against a tree a short distance away. In her excitement to join Mother, she had not paid attention to the things Father had carried in the sack.

Panic shot through her. Her gut started to scream. Mother wasn't coming! He had brought them here to hurt them. Far into the woods where no one would hear a sound. He looked at her. She knew that he knew. *She must move fast.* If she could quickly get to the rifle before he had time to react, she could save them.

The second he looked away, she leaped to her feet and darted toward the rifle. But he was too quick. He sprang to his feet and grabbed it before she could reach it and she stumbled backwards and fell to the ground.

"Not fast enough for me," he spat.

Kelly looked at him, more fearful than she had ever felt before. This was it. She just knew it. She closed her eyes tight and whispered, "Oh Mother. Where are you?"

"Where is she?" he asked, hearing her plea. "She's where she belongs! Where all the sinners go. Where you all belong!"

Tears welled up in her eyes. Angrily, she screamed, "You killed our mother, didn't you?!"

He scoffed. "She killed herself! The moment she took to another man she dug her own grave. And you three are just like her. You can't be trusted!"

"So, you are going to kill us?" Kelly asked, in anguish. She could hear a low, tortured whine behind her coming from the children.

"I can't keep taking care of ya's. Especially now that you brought that boy around. This is all your fault, girl."

The sun was just beginning to rise through the trees. She could make a run for it but knew that the odds of all three of them escaping would be impossible. She glanced around in desperation. It was then that she noticed a large hole dug in the earth around twenty yards away. She sat horrified. *This was the end for them? This was God's plan? No!* Her mind screamed. She sat frozen, wondering what to do next when she suddenly heard the loud piercing sound of a whistle. She looked to find Billy, wide eyed, holding the red whistle that Tommy had gotten him to his lips. Father quickly leaped over and swung the rifle's barrel across his mouth. The whistle shattered and flew to the ground with Billy tumbling next to it. Blood was coming from his mouth and as Kelly was about to run to him, the sound of an engine roaring caught her attention. She stopped and turned to see the image of a man on a four-wheeler nearing them. She squinted to see who it was, and a huge sigh of relief escaped her lips. It was the sheriff from the night of the dance! Excitement and relief filled her. They would be saved after all. *Billy's whistle had saved them!* She ran to Billy and bent to console him and then looked up at Father. The look of satisfaction she wore quickly left her face when she realized that he did not seem alarmed at all. In fact, he looked relieved. And panic once again shot through her.

Sheriff Brady parked the machine, slowly got off, and walked over to them. He looked at her and then at Billy and Beth and shook his head in disgust.

"You were supposed to take care of this years ago," he finally said to Father, without taking his eyes off them. "Got a call from Owens," he continued, "Said his boy was missing. You had best get this takin' care of. I can't keep cleaning up your messes. Been doing it my whole life."

"I don't need your help!" Father spat at him.

"Oh, you've always needed your big brother's help. You're stupid! A coward! Pa's probably pissing on ya from the grave. Been cleanin' up after you since the day you were born. I told you not to marry that whore to begin with. And who cleaned up that mess for ya? She was just like Ma. Nothing but a whore."

He walked over and snatched the rifle from Father's hands. Father fearfully recoiled but said nothing. Brady checked to make sure that the rifle was loaded and then slowly pointed it at Kelly.

"Guess we'll start with the oldest and work our way down," he said, void of any emotion.

Kelly stood in horror. She decided she would not make this easy for them. She quickly charged the Sheriff with full force causing him to stumble backwards and fall to the ground, landing hard on the tree log. She too lost her balance and tumbled next to him. The rifle flew from his hands and landed a few feet away. He let out an agonizing grunt and laid there as if paralyzed, grasping at his back. She quickly got up on all fours and proceeded to crawl as fast as she could to reach the rifle. Just as she was about to grab it, father kicked her hard in the jaw which sent her reeling backwards. He reached down and grabbed the rifle. With blood oozing from her mouth, she managed to stumble to her feet and was now charging *him* with full force. Father lifted the rifle to her and pulled the trigger. A deafening gunshot rang out. And to her horror she saw Billy drop before her. He had leaped in front of her to shield her with his body. Her head became dizzy and heavy air pounded in her ears as she stood there frozen. Beth's scream finally brought her to her senses, and she watched her little sister run and throw herself upon Billy's bloodied body. Still stunned, Kelly glared at her father. And with unbridled power she never knew she possessed, she charged him once again and this time they both fell to the ground.

The rifle fell from his hands and landed on the ground. They desperately began to wrestle to retrieve it. With uncontrolled frenzy, Kelly dug her fingers deep into his eyes. He yelled out in pain and frantically pried her hands free from his face. He reached over and blindly found a rock, grabbed a hold of it with one hand and swung it hard, striking her on the side of the head. It sent her reeling sideways and blood began pouring from the wound. He scrambled to his feet and turned to retrieve the rifle once again. But it was gone. In a panic, he turned. Through blurry vision from the blood seeping into her eyes, Kelly could see the rifle in Beth's tiny hands. Both Brady, who was still having trouble getting up off the ground, and Father, who was standing near him, froze.

"Give me the gun, child," Father finally said, in a low cautious voice. She did not budge. He took a step toward her and another shot fired. Kelly saw Father drop before her and everything went black.

CHAPTER 24

It was two in the morning when Chris and Tommy got to the Owens residence. Pete and Nancy rushed out the door when they pulled into the driveway.

"Dad!" Tommy yelled, as he got out of the truck. "This is Chris," he said, breathlessly. "He knows all about Kelly and how crazy her father is. We need to get there now!"

"Okay, Tom," Pete said, relieved to have his son home and safe. "I'll give Brady a call and demand we go back there."

"Now!" Tommy insisted.

"Okay," Pete agreed. "Let me call him and we'll wait until he gets here."

"I'm not waiting, Dad!" he insisted as he hurried to the barn to retrieve his four-wheeler.

"Son, that's too dangerous! Especially if he's as crazy as you say!" Pete yelled.

Tommy ignored him. He jumped on the four-wheeler and started it. Suddenly, he felt a body squeeze on the back. He turned to see Chris. "I'm going too," he stated. They backed out of the barn and spun off into the dark woods as Pete ran into the house to call Sheriff Brady.

They drove feverishly to Kelly's house and hopped off the four-wheeler, grabbing two flashlights from the cargo box. The pickup was in the driveway, but the house was dark throughout. Tommy went to the back basement window and bent down to find that it was still broken. He shined his flashlight through the window and around the basement. He did not see Kelly or the kids. In a panic, he ran to the front of the house and began pounding on the front door. No one came. Seeing that the lock was gone, he turned the handle, and the door opened. Once inside, he turned on a light and he and Chris proceeded to search for Kelly and the kids. They found no one upstairs so they scurried to the basement. It was empty. Tommy ran to the hiding spot and threw the plywood aside and peered in. Still nothing

"They have to be in the woods!" he yelled to Chris and together they ran back outside and were once again on the four-wheeler. With desperation, they sped around the woods for what seemed like an eternity, stopping now and again to listen for any kind of clue that might lead them to the children.

The sun was beginning to peer through the trees. Tommy stopped the machine, turned off the engine and sat, feeling defeated. Chris got off, put his hands on his hips and hopelessly scanned the woods. Then he looked back at Tommy and with pain in his eyes, sadly said, "I lost them again." As Tommy was about to respond, they heard the faint sound of a whistle blowing off in the distance. Chris hopped back onto the machine. They sat and frantically looked around for a few minutes, trying to decipher where it might have come from. Just then, the sound of gunfire pierced the silent woods. And they were off and flying through the trees again, heading toward the gunfire.

It wasn't long after that a second shot rang out that they finally spotted the image of a man and a young child off in the distance. As they raced toward the scene, they spotted Sheriff Brady holding onto Beth's arm and the bodies of others lying scattered about. Tommy floored the machine to them and nearly rolled it over as he skidded to a sudden halt. He jumped off and ran to Kelly who was lying on the ground.

"I got this under control!" Sheriff Brady yelled with heavy breaths and in obvious pain. He held his pistol in one hand and was grasping Beth's arm tightly with the other. "I called for an ambulance."

Ignoring him, Tommy softly touched Kelly's bloodied face and she let out a small cough. He quickly tore his shirt off, gently propped her head up, and wrapped it around the wound.

Chris saw Billy lying on the ground, motionless, with a large hole in his abdomen. He let out a horrifying groan and ran to him. He bent down, and he too, quickly removed his shirt to press it into the bullet wound in an attempt to stop the bleeding. Billy's heart was still beating and his opened eyes stared blankly into space. Chris reached out to cradle him in his arms. He gently brushed his hair aside and his own heart almost stopped. Looking into Billy's eyes, he could see his own.

"My boy," Chris softly whispered to him. He stared at him for a moment to soak in every detail of his face before leaning down to place a soft kiss on his forehead. When he lifted his head, Billy's eyes slowly moved to look directly into his. An indescribable look of peace seemed to wash over his face as if he too could feel the bond.

Neither Tommy nor Chris cared to look at Charlie's lifeless body.

"Beth…" Kelly finally spoke, barely audible. Tommy looked over to Beth and Sheriff Brady. "Beth!" he panted and gently laid Kelly's head down to go to her. She was clearly in shock and stood motionless as she stared down at Billy. Chris left Billy's side, and he too went to Beth. They both bent down and wrapped an arm around her to comfort her.

And it was then that they heard a click. They both turned, looked up, and froze when they saw Sheriff Brady pointing his pistol at them.

"You made a bad choice coming here," he said to them with a snarl. "Should have minded your business from the start." He stretched the pistol out and pointed it at Tommy's head. Without taking his eyes off them, he nodded towards Tommy's four-wheeler.

"Looks like Daddy didn't waste any time fixin' that for ya. Things happen for a reason, ya know. Should have left it alone. Well, he's not gonna be able to fix this."

Tommy closed his eyes. He silently prayed to the God that he had not taken much stock in since Bella's death. And it was then that Chris leaped up to shove Brady's arm away, but not before another shot rang out. Chris and Tommy stood frozen as Brady fell forward. Blood began spewing from his back. Chris quickly picked Beth up and carried her a good ten feet away before setting her back down. He and Tommy scanned the woods in a panic, searching for where the shot had come from. And then Tommy spotted the image of a tall man off in the distance, donned in hunting gear, turning to duck back behind the trees. The hunter glanced back only once at Tommy, until finally disappearing into the thick woods. But before he was completely out of sight, Tommy couldn't help but notice his gait. It was a gait that carried a limp.

Tommy quickly ran back to Kelly and bent to check on her. She was still weak and groggy but managed to utter a few more words to him. "She's not coming. Mother's not coming."

"It's gonna be okay," Tommy said softly and reached out to cradle her in his arms again.

"We got to get these two to a hospital," Chris said desperately. "You go for help, and I'll stay with them."

Just as Tommy was about to hop back on his four-wheeler, they heard the sound of a group of engines speeding through the woods and heading towards them. Pete, along with three State Troopers, raced up to them and jumped off two ATV's.

"Medics are on the way!" one of the Troopers yelled as he ran to Billy first.

And no sooner had he said it that two rescue ATVs rushed into sight and raced toward the scene. Once there, they wasted no time treating the gruesome scene they discovered before them.

Tommy turned to Pete and as he struggled for words, Pete threw his arms around him. Tommy laid his head on his father's shoulder and began to weep, uncontrollably. Pete gently rubbed his back and whispered, tenderly, "It's okay, Son. It's gonna be okay. Got a call from Mr. Bradshaw, strangely, right after you left. 3 o'clock this morning. He wanted to let me know to call the state police if we needed help. Not Brady. And then he got confused and wasn't sure who he was talking to. But I followed his advice anyway. And thank God, I did."

When Tommy was able to compose himself, he lifted his head, nodded to his father and then looked over at Beth. Chris had her in his arms as he was trying to tell the troopers what had happened.

"And what about the Sheriff?" one of the trooper's asked. "How did he get shot?"

Chris shrugged his shoulders in confusion and looked towards Tommy for an answer. The troopers did the same.

Tommy hesitated for a moment and then finally answered. "I don't know. I'm guessing a stray bullet."

"A *stray?*" one of the trooper's asked, incredulously.

"I know it's turkey season, but what are the odds of that?" the other asked, doubtfully. "You didn't see *anything*?"

"Nope," Tommy replied, flatly and then looked at Chris with an expression that begged him to leave it alone. Chris raised his eyebrows momentarily at him, but didn't say a word. *He left it alone.*

CHAPTER 25

Kelly sat with a mound of bandages wrapped around her head. The hospital room was cold and even with the heavy wool blanket that the nurse had draped over her legs, she was still shivering. Tommy sat on the edge of the bed next to her, glancing at Chris and Nancy from time to time as they sat in the surrounding chairs silently trying to grasp the reality of what had happened. They had been there all morning and there was still no word on Billy's condition.

"Would you like to sit with me?" Nancy asked Beth, who was staring out the window and quietly humming to herself.

Beth did not respond. Kelly was just as worried about her as she was Billy. Her face was snow white and she had not spoken a word since they arrived at the hospital. All she had managed was the eerie humming that softly dripped from her mouth that precariously sounded like doom.

Tommy looked at Kelly and then gently took her hand and held it in his. She looked back at him, sadly, and whispered, "Mother never came, Tommy."

"I know," he said. "I'm sorry."

"All these years," she continued, and looked down. "And I believed him. And I put the children through this. I should have known better. I should have saved us from him."

"Kelly, you were a child, too. None of this is your fault. He was a sick man."

A long sigh escaped her lips. "But you found Chris," she said and looked in his direction.

"I did," he said softly, "And you need to know that he never forgot about you. He loves you, Kelly. And he loved your mother." That made her smile. "And he loves Beth and Billy," he continued.

"He knows Billy?" she asked, confused.

He glanced at Chris and then back to Kelly and cautiously replied. "There are things you need to know. And we will tell you everything, but right now you need to concentrate on getting better."

Their conversation was interrupted when Pete walked into the room carrying a cardboard tray of coffees and hot chocolate.

"Any news on the boy?" he asked.

"Not yet," Chris replied. "'Doctors' have been in there all morning."

Pete shook his head in dismay, handed out the drinks, and squatted down next to him.

"Johnson's dead," he began, quietly, so that the others wouldn't hear. "Sheriff's in critical condition with guards at his door. The feds' been digging all morning and their dogs came across three graves so far."

Chris raised his eyebrows with surprise. "*Three?*"

Pete reluctantly nodded his head and continued, "The one corpse was pretty decomposed. They're gonna send it to forensics but the obvious guess is it's Camille Johnson."

Chris dropped his eyes and slowly shook his head.

"The other two were fairly new graves," Pete continued, "Troopers said they look like strangulations. The one looks like a young girl. They're guessing it might be that Melanie Burrows that went missing a couple weeks ago. She never made it home. And the other grave, they're not sure yet. They're gonna have to go through missing person reports. She still had all her clothes on though, right down to a pair of bright, red shoes. Makes me sick to my stomach that all this went on and nobody knew."

"Except for the one person who could've stopped it," Chris quietly added with an angry tone. "If he survives, I pray his cell mates give him what he deserves. And as for that bastard Johnson, I only wish I were the one who had put the bullet in him."

"Yeah," Pete agreed, with sympathy, and then continued. "The troopers put in a call to social services. They're contacting foster homes right now for the girls. They have an aunt, Carol Johnson, but she's in a hospital farther upstate."

"A hospital?"

"Psychiatric."

Chris slowly nodded his head in understanding.

"And apparently," Pete continued, "Brady's an uncle. Guess he legally changed his name. But we all know that he will *never* be an option for the girls, whether he lives or not."

"What about Camile's family?"

"They tracked down the grandparents. They haven't returned any calls, so I'm guessing they don't want anything to do with the kids."

"That doesn't surprise me," Chris said and shook his head with disgust.

"Anyway," Pete continued, "They're not sure if they're gonna be able to keep the girls together if they get placed in foster care."

Nancy overheard this and suddenly shot Pete with a look of panic. She kept her eyes fixed on him with an unspoken plea. Pete returned her stare and shrugged his shoulders in a state of perplexity.

Noticing this, Chris stood abruptly and motioned for Pete to follow him out of the room. As they were about to exit, they were stopped in the doorway by a young doctor who was about to make his way in. Everybody, except Kelly, stood in anticipation. She stayed in bed like she had been ordered to do, and while looking at the doctor, she suddenly found it hard to breathe. The air in the room seemed to thicken and choke her and she began to gasp for air. Tommy immediately sat down on the bed next to her and wrapped his arm around her to pull her close. His touch instantly soothed her, and she took in a deep, unsteady, breath and slowly let it out, allowing the tenseness to flow from her body.

The doctor glanced at her momentarily and then slowly walked into the room and put his head down for a moment before looking back up at them.

"I'm sorry," he finally said. "He didn't make it."

The room exploded with a deafening silence as they all tried to comprehend his words. Even Beth's humming had stopped as she turned to face him.

It was Chris who was the first to react. He closed his eyes and let out an agonizing groan. His shoulders slumped and he grasped his forehead with both hands. Tears began to stream down his face and that's when the realization struck Kelly as to what the doctor had just said. A slow, painful, high-pitched whine escaped her mouth before she crumpled into Tommy's arms and buried her head deep into his chest. He held on to her tightly as her body shook with each uncontrollable silent sob. Fighting back his own tears, he glanced around. The entire room had become engulfed with such intense sadness that no one could seem to find any words.

All except for Beth. She marched over and stared at Kelly with anger and confusion. Then she scanned the room in bewilderment.

"I want to see Billy," she finally demanded, turning to glare at the doctor. Nancy went to reach for her, but she pulled away.

"Where's Billy?!" she cried out. Chris bent down to her and gently took her hands in his. "Beth…your brother is gone."

"Where?" she demanded.

He hesitated for a minute and stared sorrowfully into her eyes. "He has gone to live with the angels," he said softly. Beth stared at him with wide eyes and then became even more angry. She snatched her hands from him.

"Then I want to go to the angels too!" she screamed. "He needs me with him!" He leaned in to console her, but she continued to back away.

"No!" she yelled.

He reached out again and was able to finally pull her into his arms. She frailed and kicked, but he held on tightly until she at last collapsed and released the most torturous wail. In anguish, Kelly looked at Tommy and with tears flowing down her face, managed to mutter, "I want to go to the angels, too." He wrapped his arms tighter around her. "No, Kelly, I need you here. And Beth needs you here. We *all* need you here."

***

As Chris entered the operating room to say goodbye, he saw the sheet draped over Billy's delicate four foot frame. It seemed too small, and he had to wonder if it was, indeed, him even under that sheet.

He slowly approached and gently pulled the sheet back to view his face. Adoration, mixed with pain, washed over him. There he was. His beautiful child. The child he had never gotten the chance to know. Everything about him, other than his blond hair, bore his own resemblance.

He reached his hand up and brushed the tuffet of hair lying on his closed eyes to the side. He remembered those eyes beneath the lids. How they looked into his own as he laid there in the woods, fighting for life. How they were, undeniably, the resemblance of his eyes.

"Son," he began. "I pray that your soul can hear me because there is so much I need you to know." He paused and cleared the lump in his throat. "I have always felt you, but I wish that I had known you. I should have been the one raising you. I should have protected you. I'm sorry for not fighting for you harder and I will regret that for the rest of my life." He frowned and put his head down before looking back at him. "Tommy says you were very protective of your sisters." He smiled at him. "I would have guessed that. You're my boy. Just know that I will do my best to protect them as well. And I will never forget you. *Ever.* You were created by a love that still dwells deep within my heart. A love that most are not lucky enough to find. I know that you are with your mother now, where all the beautiful souls go, and I am certain that she is holding you happily in her arms. I love you, Son."

He tenderly placed a kiss on his forehead, placed the sheet back over his face and looked up and said out loud, "Take care of our boy, Camille."

CHAPTER 26

Kelly put on the dress that Nancy had bought for her and looked in the mirror. It was black and the velvet material flowed down just below her knees. It looked rather sophisticated, but Kelly felt anything but that. In fact, she felt like a little girl again. This was the morning that they would all dress up and head to the cemetery to say their final goodbyes to Mother and Billy.

She headed out of her bedroom and popped her head in to check on Beth. Beth was struggling with the tights that Nancy had laid out for her.

"Ugg!" Beth yelled and kicked her feet in frustration.

"Let me help," Kelly said and walked in to tug and adjust the tights that were twisted awkwardly around her legs.

"I don't want to go to a cemetery," Beth complained. "Why do we have to go there?"

"Chris says it's important," Kelly explained to her. "We need to say goodbye to Billy and Mother properly. For us and for them."

"Well, I think it's dumb. Especially for Billy. I still see him alot and I don't need to say goodbye."

The comment made Kelly uneasy. She did not know if this was normal behavior, but if it helped Beth, she would leave it alone.

"Girls!" Pete yelled up the stairs. "Are you almost ready?"

"Yes!" Kelly yelled down and then continued to hurry Beth along.

When they finally made it down the stairs, Pete, Nancy, and Tommy were all waiting and together they headed out the door.

***

They made their way to the cemetery and Chris and JoAnne were already there waiting for them. A few other people were standing nearby as well, but Kelly did not know who they were. The air was cold, and even with the heavy wool coat and scarf that she was wearing, she still felt chilled. Chris walked over to hug her tightly and then leaned down to do the same for Beth.

"Thank you for letting me do this," he said and gave her a sad smile.

Kelly nodded and took Beth's hand. She glanced over and could see the two stones that were etched with Mother and Billy's names on them. She had been told that they were cremated, and when she asked what that meant, her stomach turned. She did not want to think that they were now simply ashes. This was meant to be a place where they could come to talk to them, she was also told. But Kelly didn't need this place. She had talked to Mother for years in her heart and she would continue to do so in the future. And she would do the same with Billy.

A steady rain began to fall. *God is crying.* Her mind wandered to a memory. She was leaning over the back of the couch with a scowl watching the rain beat against the front windowpane.

"Why does it have to rain?!" she complained. *"I want to go to the park."*

Mother came and nestled beside her and looked out the window. *"God is crying,"* she had said.

"But why?"

"Sometimes the burden gets too heavy. The tears take the sorrow and pain away so that you can feel better. Like taking a bath, only on the inside."

Kelly thought about this and then felt satisfied with her answer.

"Well, I hope God feels better tomorrow."

Mother smiled and squeezed her tight.

"Kelly…Kelly," Tommy said, interrupting her thoughts.

He stood next to her and held an umbrella over her head. She glanced around and watched as all the other umbrellas popped open in unison.

"Perhaps we should start the service," a tall, older man wearing a black trench coat announced while holding his own umbrella in one hand and a bible in the other. They all moved in closer as he began with a prayer. "Our Father in heaven…" and that was all Kelly heard as she turned to see Beth crouched down beside Billy's stone. The rain was causing water to splash up on the stone, and Beth was unsuccessfully trying to wipe it dry with her hand. Nancy was trying to coax her to get back under her umbrella, but she would not listen. Kelly left Tommy's side and went to kneel down beside her.

"Beth, it's cold. You need to get back under the umbrella."

"I don't want to."

"I know but you're gonna get sick."

"So, what. Billy's rock is getting wet."

Kelly let her continue for a moment longer. "Those are God's tears," she assured her. "God is sad for Billy, like we are."

But Beth did not look sad. In fact, she had not seen her shed a single tear since that awful moment that the doctor had told them that Billy was gone. It confused her and she had mentioned this to Tommy. He assured her that everybody had their own way of grieving and Beth would have to find her own way to get through this.

Beth looked up at her, curiously. "If God was gonna be sad, why did he take him?"

Kelly couldn't answer this. She often wondered about these things as well, but she trusted that He had his reasons.

By now Tommy had walked over and placed his umbrella over both their heads. Kelly stood up and reached her hand down.

"Come on, Beth. Come stand with us."

Beth obeyed and rose to join Tommy and Kelly under the umbrella. The service continued for a while longer and by the time the pastor had finished his eulogy, the rain had stopped.

"We're gonna have a little luncheon back at the house afterwards," Pete announced to the group. "Everyone is welcome."

Tommy turned to Kelly. "I'll be right back," he said to her and then headed towards the car.

Two of the people that Kelly did not recognize slowly walked up to the stones and bowed their heads. They were an elderly couple that had a refined and sophisticated air about them. The man, who wore a very polished black suit, seemed a little annoyed as he stared down at Mother's stone. The woman, who was also exquisitely dressed in a pair of black leather boots that reached up to touch the bottom of her mahogany mink coat, held a different expression. She seemed rather distraught as she nervously glanced at Kelly from time to time. Kelly still did not know who they were, but she was pleased that they probably cared about Mother and Billy. Even if the woman's stares made her uneasy, she was glad that they were here.

They finally backed away when Tommy and Chris approached the stones. Tommy bent down next to Billy's grave and set a soccer ball next to his stone. Kelly's heart immediately melted, and a tear formed in her eye. They had been told that they could bring something to set next to the stones, but she could not think of one thing to summarize their lives. But Tommy's gift was perfect. She did not know that he had planned to do this and it made her happy. The day that they had played soccer in the woods was certainly one of Billy's favorite days. She looked at Beth and smiled. Beth returned the smile and then went over and wrapped her arms around Tommy and squeezed him tightly.

Then it was Chris's turn. He went to Mother's stone and gently laid a bundle of daisies next to it. He picked out a single daisy from the bunch and laid it next to Billy's stone. Once again, Kelly's heart climbed into her throat, but she managed to smile anyway. It was perfect. Both gifts were perfect. She couldn't help but feel that no matter how sad her life had been and how much had been taken from her, she had been given two wonderful men. Well, three, including Pete. And that's how Mother would have felt. She wanted to always be like Mother. She, *too*, will always manage to smile.

When the funeral service had finally come to an end, Tommy took Kelly and Beth's hand to lead them back to the car. As they approached, Kelly noticed a white van parked in front of the car that had not been there when they arrived. Next to the van, a man stood, donned in white clothing covered by a heavy, navy coat. He had his hands resting on the handles of a wheelchair where a middle-aged woman sat. She wore sunglasses, even though the skies were overcast, a silk scarf around her hair and a heavy blanket was draped around her shoulders. As they neared her, she took the sunglasses off and stood up, letting the blanket drop from her shoulders and fall onto the chair. She stared intently at Kelly until Kelly felt forced to stop as if strangely drawn to this woman.

"Kelly…" Tommy said cautiously.

She ignored him and continued over to the woman. The woman gave her a melancholic smile when she reached her. Something was oddly familiar about her.

"My God," the woman spoke. "You are the splitting image of your Momma."

The woman then reached out and pulled Kelly into her arms and hugged her tightly. Kelly did not resist. She felt an immediate, unexplained bond with this woman.

"Sweet, baby girl," the woman murmured as she gently rocked her in her arms.

"Kelly?" Beth asked, from behind her, causing the woman to take a step back. She then looked at Beth and smiled again.

"You girls are absolutely beautiful," she praised as she bent slightly to lay her hand on Beth's cheek.

"Who are you?" Beth asked.

"I'm your Aunt Carol," she replied softly.

Kelly's mind quickly flashed back.

"Get out! You are not welcome here!" Father had yelled.

"You're sick. You need help!"

He reached out to grab Aunt Carol by the throat...

Kelly shook her head to clear the image from her mind. She stared at Aunt Carol, studying every detail of her face. It seemed to carry much pain and looked rather worn. She didn't know much about her, but she knew that this woman was carrying a world of sorrow on her shoulders as well.

"Not much longer, Ms. Johnson," the man behind her said.

Aunt Carol nodded her head and then reached in her pocket and pulled out a small white card.

"Here," she said and handed it to Kelly. "This is my address. Please write to me. And my doctor's name is on here. I think he can help you."

Kelly took the card and placed it in her pocket. Aunt Carol warmly touched her cheek one more time and then turned, and with difficult mobility, walked back to the van. The man in white opened the door to the backseat and helped her in. He then folded the wheelchair, opened the back doors, and stowed it away before getting in the driver's seat.

As the van pulled away, Aunt Carol placed her fingertips on the window and stared sorrowfully at Kelly. Kelly waited until the van was out of sight before she turned to Tommy. "I'd like to leave now," she said, depleted of emotion.

***

When they arrived back at the house, Beth quickly ran upstairs to her bedroom to take her tights off. Kelly followed her up and headed to her own bedroom to look for the thick, wool sweater that Nancy had given her. The morning had taken a toll on her, leaving her feeling drained and chilled and her stomach seemed a bit unsettled. She could already hear the chatter downstairs as the kitchen filled with the others and she dreaded having to go back down. She would have much rather just crawled back into bed and buried herself under the covers to silently reflect on the two lives that had been taken from her. But she knew that if she didn't go back down, it would cause Tommy and Nancy concern, so she put the sweater on and headed out.

As she passed Beth's room, she could see her sprawled face down on her bed with the tights balled up and lying on the floor. She went in and sat down on the bed beside her and gently rubbed her back.

"You okay?" she asked her.

Beth turned her head to look at her and nodded.

"You coming down? There's a lot of pastries down there."

Beth shrugged her shoulders.

"You don't have to," Kelly said, quietly. "Rest for a while and come down later."

Beth nodded her head in agreement and Kelly bent down to kiss her on the head before leaving the room to head out.

As she made her way downstairs, she could hear voices coming from the kitchen along with the smell of coffee brewing. She entered hoping to find Tommy, but instead found Nancy, JoAnne, and the pastor. JoAnne and Nancy were busy arranging fruit, banana bread, and danishes on a platter while the pastor rambled on about Oxville's history. Nancy looked up at Kelly and her eyes widened with concern. She appeared to be distraught but said nothing.

"You must be Kelly," the pastor said as he looked at her and smiled.

"Yes," she said, and feigned a smile back.

"I'm sorry for all you've gone through. I hope you find comfort knowing that your loved ones are now resting in the arms of God."

She nodded her head. She did not feel like talking. *Where was Tommy?*

"Are you hungry?" Nancy asked.

The thought of food on top of her already unsettled stomach made her grimace.

"That would be a no," JoAnne laughed.

"You don't even know them!" she suddenly heard Chris say with a raised voice from the dining room.

Kelly caught Nancy glancing at JoAnne with alarm in her eyes and then back to her. Confused, Kelly walked toward the dining room and peered around the corner. Chris, Pete, and Tommy were standing in the room with the elderly couple from the cemetery.

She quickly stepped back behind the wall to shield herself from their view.

"They're our grandchildren," the man said.

Nancy continued to glance at her as she nodded her head in agreement with the pastor, but it was obvious that she was not listening to one word he was saying.

"These girls have been through enough," Pete said. "We were fortunate enough to be granted temporary custody. And we plan on seeking full custody."

"Children should be with blood," the man continued.

"Blood?" Chris retorted with exasperation. "You mean like Camille's blood? You pushed that blood clear out of your lives!"

"Camille made her own choices!" the man quickly retorted. "She severed the bond the second she slept with that man. And she didn't give one thought about dragging our family name through the mud!"

"She was raped!" Chris spat, angrily.

The woman closed her eyes, and her shoulders dropped.

"Kelly," Nancy tried as she attempted to pull her away from the wall.

Kelly yanked her arm away and continued to stand and listen to the conversation taking place in the dining room.

"Raped?" the man asked doubtfully. "They were dating. I find it hard to believe it was rape."

"You find it hard to believe a man capable of murder is not capable of *rape*?" Chris asked, bewildered. "Shame on you! Shame on you both. You hand fed your daughter to a monster!"

"I've heard enough," the man said and began to leave. His wife was quick to follow and together they strode through the kitchen to head towards the foyer. He glanced at Kelly on his way through, but there was no warmth in his eyes. His wife, on the other hand, stopped and looked desperately into her eyes. Kelly did not know how to react. She knew nothing about this woman and felt no connection.

"Come on, Doris," he commanded, and she quickly turned and moved swiftly to catch up to him.

Pete, Chris, and Tommy followed them to the foyer with Kelly, Nancy, and JoAnne close at their heels.

"I will be filing for guardianship," the man said as he pulled his coat from the coat rack and slid it on.

"You don't even know who they are!" Tommy shouted in a panic.

The man stopped and looked at him with disgust. "You're the boyfriend, aren't you? An underage girl is allowed to shack up with her boyfriend. I'm sure the judge would love to know this."

"It's not like that!" Pete yelled in anger as Nancy quickly wrapped her arms around Kelly in an attempt to shield her from any shame.

"Underage?" Chris cut in. "Tell us, do you even know how old these girls are?'

The man stared hard at him.

"I didn't think so," Chris finished.

The man took the woman's mink off the coat rack and draped it around her. "You'll be hearing from us," he continued. "As soon as the judge grants us custody, we will be taking these girls to live with us in Syracuse."

"*These girls* have names!" Nancy suddenly shouted with tears in her eyes. She squeezed Kelly tighter and looked desperately at the woman. A look of pity crossed the woman's face as she dropped her gaze to the floor.

"I'm not living in Silacuse!" they heard Beth shout as she came running down the stairs. She ran to Tommy and threw her arms around his waist. "Tell them, Tommy. Tell them we are gonna stay with you."

"It's okay, Beth," Tommy assured her as he glared at the man. "Nobody's going anywhere."

"We'll see about that," the man said as he showed himself and his wife out.

The door shut and they all stood silent for a minute.

"I should have never called them," Chris finally said quietly.

JoAnne quickly went to his side and put an arm around him.

"Who were those people?" Beth finally asked.

"Just a couple strangers," Kelly said without emotion and looked down at her.

"Well, I don't like them," Beth responded and then left to go to the kitchen to get a pastry.

Tommy looked pleadingly at Pete. "What are we gonna do, Dad?"

Pete sighed. "Don't worry, Son. I'll make some calls."

Tommy went to Kelly's side and took her hands. He could see the worry on her face and wanted so badly to reassure her that they had nothing to worry about and that she would never have to leave this house to live with people she didn't know. But he couldn't.

CHAPTER 27

Kelly awoke and sat up. Her body felt good all over. For the first time in the month that had passed, she slept through an entire night uninterrupted by cries coming from the bedroom next door. Beth's nightmares had slowly become less intense and last night proved that they may have finally come to an end. Kelly's nightly comfort and reassurance that no one would ever hurt them again seemed to have finally convinced Beth that they were safe. And now she would have to work on convincing herself.

A gleam of sunlight peering through a crack in the curtains caught her eye. She stretched, pulled the thick comforter from her body, and climbed out of bed. She pushed the curtains aside and took a full look out the window. A beautiful blanket of sparkling snow covered the ground and off in the distance, a doe and two fawns bounced playfully across the lawn. She smiled as a sense of peace washed over her. She closed her eyes and softly whispered, "Good morning, God."

The aroma of bacon frying caught her senses. She eagerly left the window and rushed to throw on her robe and slippers to head downstairs. As she descended the long, curving staircase, she suddenly stopped and stood in awe. There at the bottom, in the corner of the large family room, stood the most glorious Christmas tree she could ever imagine. Although she had helped hang all the shiny ornaments and popcorn garland, seeing it this morning, all lit up with brilliant, dancing, colorful lights, took her breath away. Big and small cleverly decorated packages were scattered around the base of the tree.

She stood there and stared, taking it all in. She thought of Mother. Oh, how she would have loved this sight. She thought of Billy. He had never seen this sight. So much had been taken from them. She swallowed hard as her throat welled up.

Her thoughts were interrupted by the sound of soft footsteps behind her. She turned to find Beth, wide eyed, also staring down at the tree. Her cheeks were rose colored, and her long blonde curls glistened from the sun's rays that shone brightly through the large bay windows. She slowly looked up at Kelly with her mouth agape and wonderment in her eyes. Kelly smiled at her and answered her unspoken question. "Yes, Beth…this is Christmas."

"Good morning, girls!" called Pete, as he entered the room below and grinned brightly up to them. "Merry Christmas! Breakfast is in the works!"

Kelly and Beth scurried down the stairs, smiling widely. Beth ran to the tree and plopped down in front of it to touch the pretty packages. Kelly strolled into the kitchen where Nancy and Tommy were busy stirring pancake batter and frying bacon.

"Can I help?" she asked.

"I think we have it all under control, but thank you," Nancy said, "Relax and enjoy your morning."

"Yeah, we got this," Tommy chimed in, grinning from ear to ear. He rolled up a kitchen towel and playfully threatened to snap her with it. "Now get on outta here!"

Kelly giggled and bounced out of the kitchen to join Beth on the living room floor. Beth nestled against her and after a few minutes, asked innocently, "Do you think Billy can see us?"

Kelly gave her a squeeze. "I think he can."

"I feel bad." Beth continued. "It's not fair that he can't share all of this with us."

Kelly thought for a moment. "I'm sure there is Christmas in Heaven. It's Jesus's birthday, after all! And I know Billy would not want you to feel bad. He loved you so much. He would want you to be happy, Beth."

Beth smiled and they snuggled even closer together until they were interrupted by the sound of the doorbell chiming. Pete trotted over to the front door and opened it to find Chris and JoAnne smiling brightly and juggling bags full of packages.

"Merry Christmas! Make yourselves at home!" Pete insisted, as they stepped inside. "There's coffee and tea in the kitchen."

Chris and JoAnne greeted the girls as they walked past and placed the shopping bags on the floor next to the tree before heading to the kitchen. All except for one box. They had purposefully left it behind to have Pete secretly snatch it up and disappear with it.

Tommy soon joined the girls in the living room and plopped down beside them. Beth leaped to her knees to give him a big squeeze.

"It's Christmas!" she squealed.

"It is?!" he teased her, delightfully. "Geez, I better put the Halloween candy away, then!"

She laughed loudly. "Tommy, you're silly! Can't you see all these presents?"

He looked under the tree. "Oh, those?! I never noticed them!"

She giggled loudly and settled back into her sitting position. He turned to Kelly, who was sitting quietly, clearly enjoying Tommy's playful teasing.

"How about you?" he asked her. "Did you notice the presents?"

She grinned sweetly and turned to look tenderly into his eyes. "Yes, I saw them. But Tommy, what you and your family have done for us is bigger than any present under there."

He returned a smile and draped his arm around her shoulders, giving her a quick squeeze.

"Kelly, you have no idea how happy you make me. *Us.* You, *and* Beth. You both went through some horrific things and thank God you're both still here. We are all very lucky to have you in our lives."

She looked at him in awe. She could feel his sincerity, but still she knew that he could never imagine just how much he truly had done for them. And for Billy while he was still with them. His kind and generous heart had rescued them. And although Billy was brutally taken from them, Tommy had impacted his short life for the better. She loved him more than he would ever know.

The sound of the doorbell ringing again startled her from her thoughts. Pete came into the living room and looked curiously at Tommy.

"Are you expecting somebody?" he asked him.

Tommy nodded his head no and then stood up and waited for Pete to answer the door. After a short conversation, Pete opened the door wide and the elderly woman, Doris, whom they had discovered to be the girls' grandmother, stepped inside with her arms full of shopping bags. She stared at the girls as she set the bags on the floor.

"Tommy, come in the kitchen," Pete said to him.

Tommy stood confused. He looked down at Kelly who was still seated on the floor and saw that she, too, was confused. And scared. He looked back at Pete and just as he was about to voice his concerns, Pete cut in, "Please, Tom. Come with me."

He gave Kelly a sympathetic shrug and then followed Pete into the kitchen.

Kelly slowly rose to her feet and looked at the woman. Beth mimicked her and together they stood and waited, not sure of what was expected of them. Doris slowly walked to them and smiled slightly. Neither Kelly, nor Beth, returned the smile. They just stood apprehensively, waiting for some sort of explanation.

"Can we sit?" Doris asked and nodded toward the sofa.

Kelly and Beth sat on one side of the sofa and Doris took a spot on the other side. She stared at them for a moment before beginning, "You girls look so much like your mother. Especially you, Kelly."

"Are you here to take us away?" Beth asked, with a hint of anger in her voice.

Doris smiled again and then replied, "No." A tear formed in her eye, and she quickly wiped it away and took a deep breath before continuing.

"We won't be taking you children away from this, what appears to be, a very loving home. We have made too many mistakes already. I'm here to let you know that not a day goes by that I don't think about your mother. I loved her very much." She sighed, unsure of how to continue with her explanation. "You see, your grandfather was a very proud man. Still is. And I made the grave mistake of allowing him to dictate my feelings. I should have never let him send your mother away." She paused and looked at them with a glazed look. "Of course, two beautiful children came from it. I mean three," she corrected. "I'm sure Billy was just as beautiful. I only wish I could have met him." She shook her head to clear her mind and continued. "But still, I should have protected her."

Beth reached over and wiped a tear from her grandmother's eye. This evidently touched her, and she smiled as more tears fell.

"Anyway, I won't keep you girls from your Christmas celebration any longer. I just wanted to let you know how sorry I am for all that you endured." She pointed to the door. "The bags over there are for you girls. There's lots of pictures of your mother in them along with some of her favorite toys that I kept over the years. I thought you might like them."

Kelly did not respond. Of course she would love those things, but she didn't know how to talk to this newly found grandmother. She wished Tommy had been sitting with them to guide her through this conversation.

Doris glanced around at the walls and studied the pictures that hung on them. "It's a beautiful home. I'm sure you'll be happy here." And then she laughed nervously. "I'm in the market for a new place myself. Your grandfather and I are no longer together. After all these years, I'm starting over." She looked back at them. "I wouldn't mind moving closer if I knew you would allow me to be a small part of your lives someday.'

"Yes," Kelly said, quickly. "I would like that." For some odd reason, this grandmother made her feel closer to Mother and she liked the feeling.

With tears still in her eyes, Doris reached out to hug them and Kelly and Beth readily accepted the embrace. They stayed that way for a while, reveling in their newfound connection. When she finally pulled away, she stood up and went to the door to retrieve the bags and brought them back to the girls. "You can go through these on your own time," she said. "Or I can go through them with you if you'd like, in case you have any questions."

Kelly and Beth both nodded.

Just then, Pete and Nancy came into the room and looked at the girls as if to make sure that they were okay. Seemingly satisfied that they were, Pete announced that breakfast was ready. As they both rose, Beth turned to Pete and asked, "Can Grandmother have breakfast with us?"

Pete, Nancy, and Doris all lifted their eyebrows.

"Um, I suppose it would be okay," Pete said after a second and then looked at Nancy. When Nancy didn't protest, he looked back to Doris and asked, "Would you care to join us?"

Doris smiled brightly. "Thank you so much for the offer, but I have a lot of things to take care of in my life right now. I definitely plan on spending the rest of my Christmases with you in the future though. That's if you'll have me."

"Okay," Pete replied, slightly confused. "Girls, I'll meet you in the kitchen. Nancy and I would like to have a few words with Doris first."

The girls went to Doris, and each gave her a hug before heading into the kitchen.

***

169

"Before we begin," Pete announced, when they were finally all seated around the table, "I'd like to say a grace."

They all bowed their heads while Pete began, "Lord, thank you for this wonderful meal and for the wonderful family that we are blessed to share it with."

"May I add to this prayer?" Chris asked, hesitantly.

"Of, course."

He paused and swallowed hard before continuing. "And please, Lord, take care of our Billy. Keep him safe in your hands while we keep him loved in our hearts."

They all sat silent for a moment. Kelly's heart became heavy as she struggled to keep her tears at bay. After so many days of silently mourning him and Mother, she so desperately wanted to be happy on this day.

"And our Bella," Nancy suddenly added, with her eyes closed tight.

Pete and Tommy immediately raised their eyebrows, shot a look at each other, and exchanged soft smiles. She had finally spoken her name aloud and Tommy was quite certain that it was all due to the girls coming into their lives. Nancy then slowly opened her eyes, looked at each of them, and shared their smile.

"Amen!" Tommy finally announced, feeling an overwhelming sense of triumph, "Let's eat!"

They all laughed and then happily began to pass dishes around to fill their plates. They chatted and laughed all throughout breakfast, sharing amusing stories about their lives. All except for Kelly. She was quiet during the entire meal.

"Hey," Tommy finally whispered to her, "Are you okay?"

"I'm afraid," she whispered back. "Is this all real? I mean it just feels…weird."

"It is real, Kelly," he assured her. "You deserve this and so much more. It's gonna take some time but don't ever think you deserve less than this. And one day, this will be us with all ten of our own kids!"

She laughed out loud. "Tommy, shush! Are you crazy?!"

"Crazy about you," he said with a smile and then playfully reached over to snatch a piece of bacon from her plate and shove it in his mouth.

After breakfast they all headed into the family room and gathered around the tree to exchange gifts, take pictures, and drink hot cocoa. They spent the rest of the morning visiting and mostly relishing in Beth's profound excitement over all the gifts she was receiving. There were so many dolls and toys, and she refused to set any of them down until they finally spilled from her arms and scattered around her.

While everybody chuckled about the incident, Chris suddenly stood up.

"Whoa, I forgot one more gift!" he announced as he looked at Pete and winked.

Pete smiled and stood up. "I'll be right back!"

He left a confused room and then reappeared a few moments later, shielding something under his shirt panel.

"What is it?!" Beth asked, sweetly.

"Well," Chris said, "It's actually for Kelly. But I'm quite certain she'll share it."

Kelly stood up and curiously walked over to Pete. Before he could reveal what was hidden under his shirt, a small meow escaped, and her eyes lit up. As he pulled the tiny, white kitten out and placed it in Kelly's hands, a sharp quick gasp escaped both girls' mouths

She brought the kitten up to her face and gently nuzzled her cheek against his soft fur. It only took a moment for Beth to scramble to her side in delight.

"Oh, Kelly!" she squealed. "Can I hold it?"

"Him," Chris corrected.

"Him!" Beth squealed again. "Can I hold him?!"

Kelly gently placed the tiny kitten in Beth's arms.

"Oh, I love him!" she professed, delightfully.

"That little guy needs a name," Chris informed them.

Kelly thought for a moment.

"How about Christmas?" Beth asked as she looked up at Kelly.

Kelly smiled widely at her. "Why not? That sounds perfect."

"You mean *purrrfect*," Tommy chided. They all erupted in laughter.

"He still needs his shots," Chris added. "And lucky for you, there's gonna be a new vet in town!"

"What?!" Nancy, asked with excitement. "You closed on your house already?"

"Sure did!" JoAnne happily announced.

Pete looked at the girls and smiled. "Chris and JoAnne are moving to Oxville. I didn't want to say anything until it was a done deal."

Kelly's face lit up. "That's wonderful! I'm so happy!"

"So am I," Chris said, and hugged her. "So am I."

"Group hug!" Tommy yelled and they all laughed, huddled together and embraced each other until the sound of Christmas's meow announced that the hug was over, and he was hungry.

When the gift giving finally ended, Nancy, JoAnne, and Kelly headed toward the kitchen to clean up the breakfast clutter. While Nancy and JoAnne were busy clearing plates and packaging leftovers, Kelly put a plug in the sink, poured some detergent into the water and watched it slowly bubble up. And then her mind drifted.

"Just a few more minutes," Mother said and smiled. *"I want to get these dishes out of the way before we head to the park."* She was humming as she waited for the water to fill the kitchen sink.

Kelly bounced off to grab a jacket for Beth and herself. As usual Beth fussed while she tried to squeeze her arms into the jacket that seemed too small.

"Come on Beth!" Kelly complained. *"By the time I get this coat on it's gonna be winter!"*

Mother laughed and suddenly the front door swung open. They all froze as Father stomped into the kitchen and glared at Mother.

"Going somewhere?!" he thundered in his usual angry tone.

Mother stood silent for a moment and then without looking at the girls softly ordered them to go to their room. Kelly took Beth's hand and led her to her bedroom, closed the door, and plopped her on the bed. She quickly grabbed some books from the shelf and scattered them about her. As Beth began to play with the books, Kelly tiptoed back to the door and opened it slightly to get a view of the kitchen.

"Seems you can't even wait till I leave town to start running around!" he was yelling.

"I've got all my chores done. I packed your bags already. We were just gonna go…"

"Shut up!" he bellowed and then leaped at her and grabbed the back of her hair and forcefully pushed her head down into the hot, soapy water.

She struggled to free herself from his grasp but couldn't. He finally pulled her head back up and a torrent of water splashed wildly about. She coughed and gasped for air. Suds covered her wet hair, and her face was deep red.

"Please stop," she begged.

But he didn't. He shoved her head back into the water. Only this time it lasted much longer. The flailing slowed and her body began to become limp. He pulled her head back out and as she struggled to lean against the countertop, she coughed even harder and her breathing came in and out in long, deep and hoarse sounds.

"Look at me!" he shouted.

She kept her head down, still fighting for air.

"I said look at me!" he shouted again and grabbed the back of her hair again and forced her face to look at him. She pleaded with her eyes for him to stop but this only seemed to anger him more. He looked at her with disgust and then balled up his fist and slammed it into her face, causing her to scream out in pain and tumble backwards. She slid on the soapy tiles and fell hard to the floor. While she frantically tried to get to her feet, he scrambled to her and kicked hard at her body, sending her falling back to the floor. And then he did it again and again until she finally gave in and just laid there in defeat.

And then, as if nothing had happened at all, he calmly left the kitchen to head to their bedroom to retrieve his suitcase.

"That should keep you home until I get back," he calmly said when he returned. He did not look at her as she lay quietly crumpled on the floor. He headed to the door and left, slamming the door hard behind him.

"Kelly…"

"Kelly!" came Tommy's voice, snapping her from her thoughts. He reached around her and quickly turned the faucet off. The soapy water was to the top of the sink, threatening to overflow onto the countertop.

She turned to find him looking at her with bewilderment.

"Are you okay?" he asked, desperately.

She stood there speechless and trembling. He immediately reached out and pulled her to him. She collapsed in his arms and shrunk down to the floor, bringing him down with her while letting out a long, agonizing groan.

"Shh...It's gonna be okay," he calmly assured her and began to gently rock her.

And then the tears came like never before. They poured from her like Niagara Falls, releasing years of pent-up sorrow and the constant fear that her happy moments would be brutally stripped from her in a flash. She no longer had to be the strong one. She was safe. She let it all flow from her body until there was nothing left but dry, aching eyes and utter exhaustion.

It was the fifth of February and Tommy woke up not really feeling a year older, but definitely happier. He purposely slept in with the plan of skipping school for his birthday so that he and Kelly could do something special together. There was still so much that he wanted her to see and do to make up for all those years in captivity.

He someday wanted to take her to visit her Aunt Carol per her wishes, but it was still too soon. They had started writing letters to one another and Kelly would let him read them. Aunt Carol seemed to care deeply for Kelly and hoped to one day see her again. Carol's breakdown, Tommy had learned, happened the day that Kelly's grandfather Johnson had brutally murdered his wife. She had been in and out of hospitals since. She did not elaborate on the details of that day or the life she endured before it, but he was left to imagine only the worst. So for now, Tommy decided it was best to keep Kelly away from Carol while she continued to heal from her years of trauma. He knew Carol's ultimate wish was to one day be strong enough to permanently live on her own and outside of the hospital walls, but until that time, the letters would have to be enough. And although Kelly had come a long way, she still had so much more healing to do herself and he feared a visit might set her back. He desperately wanted to keep any poison from her past far from her. He *needed* to protect her.

Just thinking of Kelly motivated him to jump out of bed to start his day. He headed downstairs to the aroma of warm cinnamon rolls and bacon sizzling on the stove. Nancy was busy in the kitchen preparing the birthday breakfast she had promised him the night before. He strode in and her face immediately lit up.

"Happy Birthday!" she exclaimed and rushed over to hug him and kiss him on the cheek.

"Thanks, Mom," he said, modestly. "Where's the girls?"

"In the dining room. JoAnne agreed to come earlier this morning so that Kelly could have the rest of the day to spend with you."

"Nice," he said, as he grabbed a hot cinnamon roll from the counter and headed into the dining room.

Kelly and Beth were seated at the table with books open in front of them. JoAnne looked up at him and smiled. Nancy had hired her, at a handsome discount, to tutor the girls in the hopes of slowly catching them up to one day attend a proper school. She had a master's degree in childhood education but was in no hurry to seek employment in Oxville, as she had recently found out that she and Chris were expecting a child of their own.

"Happy birthday!" she said, brightly.

Kelly and Beth looked up from their books and immediately jumped to their feet. They scrambled to him and threw their arms around him.

"Happy birthday, Tommy!" they squealed in unison.

"Thank you…thank you," he chuckled. "How are the studies coming along?"

Kelly looked at JoAnne. "You're a great teacher, but I have to say Tommy is still my favorite."

JoAnne laughed. "That doesn't offend me in the slightest. I'm sure he was an excellent teacher."

Tommy smiled. "Okay, enough flattery. Back to work. I have big plans for today!"

"Wait!" Beth said excitedly and scurried back to the table to retrieve a piece of paper. She handed the page to him and smiled brightly. He took the paper and held it up to find a picture that she had drawn with the words Happy Birthday written at the top. The picture was a drawing of four kids, two boys and two girls, playing by a creek. Although the artwork would not have won the National Medal of Arts, it definitely captured the sweet memory of the day when he had met Kelly and the children with precise detail. Right down to their muddied faces.

"Wow," Tommy said, with sincerity. "Seems we have a budding artist in our home. I love it!" He bent to wrap his arms around her and hug her tight. She beamed with pride at the compliment and then bounced back to her seat at the table.

Kelly held up her hands. "I'm afraid I have nothing."

He grinned slyly and responded, "That's okay. You're all I need. But I wouldn't mind a little birthday kiss."

She blushed and then stood on her tippy toes to kiss him on the cheek.

Just then Nancy came into the dining room. She looked at Tommy and with a little apprehension, announced, "You have a phone call."

"Okay," he replied and reluctantly stepped away from Kelly. "Back to work!" he commanded playfully and turned to head back into the kitchen.

"Hello?" he answered, after picking up the phone.

"Happy birthday," came a sultry, familiar voice from his past.

He hesitated a moment and then finally responded, "Tanya…Thank you."

"So, it's finally here!" she exclaimed, as if nothing had changed between them at all. "You're eighteen!"

"Yea, just another year," he replied with no enthusiasm.

"Just another year? You're a legal adult now. You can do anything you want! That means you can move back to Chicago and live with Frank while we finish out our senior year. Just like we planned!"

He didn't respond.

"Tommy," she continued, with a little uncertainty. "Look, I know some time has passed between us, but I want you to know that I miss you like crazy." She paused and when he still offered no response, continued, "Okay I know about your conversation with Frank. I've made some mistakes that I truly regret and am very sorry for. That guy…that was nothing. You need to know that. It's always been you. Always has and always will."

He continued to remain silent. Months ago, he would have killed to hear these words. But now he felt no emotion. His life could not have felt more perfect than it was right now. He had Kelly. She was beyond incredible. He had his mom back. She was more than elated to have the girls in her life. And he had not seen a single sign of depression from her since the day they had moved in. His dad loved his job. Hell, even Dan had come to treat him like they were the best of friends.

"Tommy?" she asked, interrupting his thoughts. "Aren't you excited? You're finally at the age where you can have your freedom!"

"Thanks for calling Tanya." he finally answered, "I really hope you have a great life, but I'm where I want to be. Where I *belong*. I already have my freedom," he answered, confidently. "I found my freedom by the creek."

And with that, he hung up the phone, feeling nothing but complete.